THE NIGHTMARE NEXT DOOR

ALSO BY JOEL A. SUTHERLAND

The Haunted series

The Nightmare Next Door

Field of Screams

Ghosts Never Die

Night of the Living Dolls

The
Nightmare
Next Door

Joel A. Sutherland

sourcebooks
young readers

Published by Sourcebooks Young Readers, an imprint of Sourcebooks Kids
P.O. Box 4410, Naperville, Illinois 60567-4410
(630) 961-3900
sourcebookskids.com

Originally published as *Haunted: The House Next Door*
in 2017 in Canada by Scholastic Canada Ltd.

Library of Congress Cataloging-in-Publication Data

Names: Sutherland, Joel A., author.
Title: The nightmare next door / Joel A. Sutherland.
Description: Naperville, Illinois : Sourcebooks Young Readers, 2020. |
    Series: [Haunted ; book 1] | Audience: Ages 8-12. | Audience: Grades
    4-6. | Summary: "Matt and Sophie's new neighbors have made moving a
    nightmare-literally"-- Provided by publisher.
Identifiers: LCCN 2020015754 | (trade paperback)
Subjects: CYAC: Moving, Household--Fiction. | Neighbors--Fiction. |
    Ghosts--Fiction. | Horror stories.
Classification: LCC PZ7.1.S8825 Nig 2020 | DDC [Fic]--dc23
LC record available at https://lccn.loc.gov/2020015754

This product conforms to all applicable CPSC and CPSIA standards.

Source of Production: Sheridan Books, Chelsea, Michigan, United States
Date of Production: June 2020
Run Number: 5018712

Printed and bound in the United States of America.
SB 10 9 8 7 6 5 4 3 2 1

In memory of George Lenart—
the most gentle man who left the
most permanent mark.

CHAPTER 1

"LOOK ON THE BRIGHT SIDE," Dad said to my sister, Sophie, as he placed one hand on her shoulder and the other on mine, "you always wanted a horse."

Sophie sighed. "Just because there's a horse next door doesn't make it mine."

The horse was in the snowy field beside our new house. Dad, Sophie, and I had spent the afternoon unloading the rental truck and unpacking boxes, as Mom put things away. I'd walked in and out of the house dozens of times, but I hadn't noticed the horse before. It didn't make a sound or move a muscle. It stood as still as a statue. I was beginning to wonder if the horse was actually alive, but then its tail swooshed side to side, just once.

"And even if that horse was mine," Sophie continued, "I think I'd ask for my money back."

I saw her point. The horse was jet-black with a white spot on its forehead, but you'd never mistake it for Black Beauty. It was tall and should've been muscular, but its ribs were visible beneath its dull and matted coat. And I couldn't tell for sure in the dim light, but I thought I saw dark liquid trickling out of one nostril. Three of its ankles were white, while the fourth was as black as the rest of its body. I didn't know the correct term for horse ankles, but I knew Sophie would. I asked her.

"Horse ankles?" She laughed. "I think you mean pasterns, the part between the hoof and the fetlock."

I didn't bother asking what a fetlock was. Sophie knew more about horses than anyone I'd ever met, even though she was only ten and she'd never owned a horse or taken lessons. We'd gone riding for a few hours a handful of times but that was all. She's always loved horses, had loved them ever since she was old enough to say "neigh."

Dad picked a clump of tall dead grass from under the old fence that separated our new house from the rickety farmhouse next door. He held the grass over the fence and whistled through his teeth, a high, piercing sound that hurt my ears.

"Here, girl," he called to the horse, trying to entice it over. "Or boy. I don't actually know what you are. Sophie, can you tell if it's a girl or a boy?"

"I can see everything you can see from here," Sophie said. "No, I can't tell."

The horse continued to stare at us. *Swish-swish* went its tail. Otherwise it didn't move.

"What's the matter?" Dad called across the field. "Did your mommy teach you not to take grass from a stranger, or something?"

"Richard?" It was Mom. She was standing in

the front doorway behind us with a confused look on her face. "Who are you talking to?"

"Our new neighbor," Dad said.

Mom peered at the farmhouse. "New neighbor? Where?"

"There, in the field," I said, pointing. "Shadowfax."

"Nice one, Matt!" Dad said. He ruffled my hair.

"Who?" Mom said, her frown deepening.

"Shadowfax," I said. "You know, Gandalf's horse."

Dad was quick to join in the nerd fest I'd started. His voice rose as his excitement grew. "Descendant of Felaróf and Lord of the Mearas, the greatest horse bred in all of Middle-earth."

"Half of what you both just said was English and the other half was, well, I have no idea." Mom looked to Sophie for support. "Do you have any clue what they're talking about?"

"Lord of the Rings, I think," Sophie said. "But other than that, no. Not really, no."

At thirteen, I'd read the entire Lord of the Rings trilogy three times, and Dad and I had watched all the movies a dozen times together. We'd even watched the director's extended editions with hours of cut scenes added back in.

We were bona fide geeks and proud of it.

Our mother, Anne, was an auditor. Or something. I was never really sure what she did. She told me during breakfast one day, but I started thinking about the wallpaper in our kitchen, which was slightly more interesting. We had moved from Genesco to Lancaster because of her job. She got a new one in Buffalo auditing products or processes or numbers or whatever auditors audit. So we had to leave our totally awesome house to come to this bland suburban neighborhood so she could be closer to the city.

Dad was an artist, so he could work pretty much anywhere. Although painting or sketching beside the creek that flowed through our old backyard had to be better for his muse than sitting under the baking sun in our new treeless yard, listening to barking dogs and crying babies and whatever radio station the neighbors listened to while mowing their lawns.

Mom finally spotted the horse. Its black hair was like camouflage against the darkening sky. "Look at that! In all the times we came out here to check on the progress of the house I never once saw a horse. Hey, Sophie, you always wanted a horse, and now you live next door to one. Pretty cool, huh?"

Sophie looked like she was about to tell Mom the same thing she'd told Dad, but then she took a deep breath and forced a smile. "Yeah, Mom. Pretty cool."

"You never know," Mom said. "Maybe once the neighbors discover how much you love horses, they'll let you ride theirs."

I looked at the farmhouse but didn't see any sign of life other than the horse. No movement in the windows, no lights turned on, no car in the driveway. The house looked one hundred years old, easily. Maybe even older. It was as white as the snow that surrounded it. To the right of the door was a small white statue of a horse, and nearby a porch swing creaked back and forth slowly in the wind.

The other thing that caught my eye was a sign at the foot of the driveway. It read BRIAR PATCH FARM and had a silhouette of a horse in mid-run. I couldn't picture the real horse of Briar Patch Farm running like the picture of the horse on the sign—it was far too sickly looking.

Around back was a large stable that had seen better days. It used to be red, but most of the paint had peeled off the wood. I didn't think the roof had much time left before it collapsed.

The house looked stubborn. But I guess it wasn't the house that was stubborn, but whoever lived there. The old house sat surrounded on all sides by cookie-cutter homes in a newly built subdivision. All the other farmers that used to live in the area had sold their properties to developers, but not my new neighbors. They'd obviously refused to move, and now the white house with its large field, stable, and horse stood out like a sore thumb.

My family and I stared at the house in silence for a moment or two. Cold wind blew snow along the street and froze my skin. It was the first day of spring break, and I was suddenly reminded that, instead of spending the week skiing and snowboarding and skating with my friends like I'd done the past few years, I'd be spending it getting settled in my new home. Alone.

Mom shivered and hugged her arms to her body. "*Brrr.* It's cold. Let's go inside. Pizza's about ready to come out of the oven."

We all forgot about the horse—pizza, even frozen pizza, always had that effect on us—and followed my mother inside. But as we sat in a circle on the family room floor, eating cardboardy pizza off paper plates that probably tasted about the same, I happened to look out the window. It was pitch-black outside, but I thought I saw two large eyes reflecting the light from the family room. There was a shadowy blur of movement, and then the eyes were gone.

"What is it, Matt?" Mom asked.

"Nothing." I shook my head. "Nothing at all." But I had a feeling that wasn't true.

CHAPTER 2

I WOKE UP THE NEXT morning on the floor of my new room and stretched my back. It cracked loudly three times like a firecracker. *Pop, pop, pop!* Mom's yoga mat and my old sleeping bag were nowhere near as good as my actual bed. All of our large furniture was being delivered later in the day.

I got up and walked slowly to the window. Mine was the only room with a view of Briar Patch Farm.

Sophie's window looked out onto the back-yard, and Mom and Dad's faced the street. It had snowed overnight, and the ground was covered by a blanket of white powder. There was no sign of the horse, not even a single hoofprint. It must've still been in the stable.

I checked my watch. It was almost 9:30. I thought that was a little strange. I'd always heard farmers get up stupid early. The horse should have been let out of the stable by now to stretch its legs.

I pulled on the jeans from the day before and my favorite Batman T-shirt (it said WWBD? above the logo—What Would Batman Do?), and I made my way downstairs to the kitchen. Sophie and Mom were sitting on moving boxes packed with books, both holding a cereal bowl in one hand and spooning mouthfuls of Cheerios with the other.

"Morning, champ," Dad said. He stood at the counter, and although our kitchen cupboards and fridge were mostly barren, he was wearing his apron. It was black with yellow writing: COME TO THE DARK SIDE—WE HAVE COOKIES. "I'm afraid I couldn't make my traditional Sunday-morning pancakes, but can I interest you in a bowl of cereal? We have a fine selection of Cheerios, Rice Krispies, and Corn Flakes."

"Cheerios sounds good," I said, taking a seat on a third box.

"Coming right up."

"How'd you sleep?" Mom asked.

"Not too well. I miss my bed."

"Me, too," Sophie added.

"We'll sleep better tonight after the movers come," Mom said.

"You know," Dad said, handing me a bowl of cereal and a spoon, "you two kids don't need to stick around to help us today. I'm going to go grocery shopping, and your mom is going to begin unpacking. You could head out and get to know the neighborhood a little, if you'd like."

I shrugged. "If my friends were here I'd go sledding."

"So take your sister."

I turned to Sophie. "You wanna go?"

"Does a one-legged duck swim in circles?" Sophie said.

"I'll take that as a yes," I said with a laugh. Our grandpa liked weird expressions, and that one was one of his favorites—Sophie's, too.

We finished breakfast, dug our winter clothes out of moving boxes (it wasn't too difficult—Mom had labeled EVERYTHING), found our sleds in the garage, and were off.

But we stopped at the end of our driveway. We had no idea where the closest hill was.

"Um, what do you think? Right or left?" I asked.

"I don't know," Sophie said. Then she pointed across the street and said, "Look!"

Two boys had walked out of their house. They looked like marshmallows in puffy winter coats and hats and gloves, just like us. They each grabbed a sled from the side of their house, and then one of the boys spotted us.

"Hey," I said.

"Hey," the oldest boy responded. He looked about my age, and the other kid looked to be about Sophie's age.

"We just moved in," I said. "Is it cool if we follow you to the hill?"

"Sorry," the oldest boy said. "We're not going sledding."

I frowned. "Oh, um, really? It's just, you're carrying sleds, and..."

Sophie slapped my chest with the back of her hand. "They're messing with you, Matt."

I stopped talking and noticed that the boys were both smiling and laughing. "Ah, I get it," I said.

"Yeah, sure, you can come with us," the oldest boy said. "I'm Nick, and this is my little brother, Chris."

We introduced ourselves and followed them. I glanced at the farmhouse beside ours as we passed it. The blinds were drawn tight, and there was no one around. The house looked like it was hibernating for the winter.

"Have you guys lived here long?" I asked.

"We moved in October. So what's that? Four months?" Nick said.

"Five," Chris corrected. "Thanks, baby brother."

"You know I don't like it when you call me that."

"Sorry. I'll never call you *brother* again, baby." Chris sighed, but he didn't seem genuinely upset. I had the feeling they teased each other a lot, but it was all in good humor.

"How far is the hill?" Sophie asked.

"It's behind the elementary school, just up ahead—is that your new school?" Chris asked Sophie.

She nodded. I'd be going to a junior high school that was attached to the secondary school across town. But neither of us was thrilled about changing schools with only three months left in the school year.

"I go there, too," Chris continued. "Anyway, there's a forest behind the school with a path that leads to a hill. It's not huge, but there are never any little kids or parents there, so it's cool."

Just like Chris had said, we cut through the school's playground, entered a small path between some pine trees, and walked a short distance through the woods until we reached a small clearing with a hill.

"This. Is. Awesome," Sophie said.

"Wicked!" I said. I hadn't expected to find anything like it in the suburbs. It had only taken us seven or eight minutes to walk there, but it felt like we were back in the country. The forest cut off all sights and sounds from the neighborhood, and the hill wasn't as small as I'd imagined. We had the hill to ourselves, and the snow was completely undisturbed—no one had messed it up yet.

"Last one down is a rotten egg!" Sophie shouted. She flopped down on her sled and sped down the hill alone.

"Who's it gonna be?" I called and tried to catch my sister.

Chris joined me and Sophie at the bottom of the hill, and Nick, the rotten egg himself, came in last.

"You guys are weird," Nick said with a smile.

"Thank you," Sophie replied.

"You'll fit right in in this neighborhood," Chris said.

"Too soon," Nick said. "It's their first day."

Chris stood up. "Don't you think it's better they know sooner rather than later?"

Nick shrugged.

"What do you mean?" I asked. "What are you guys talking about?"

"Well, the cat's out of the bag now," Nick said. "You might as well tell them."

Chris opened his mouth, paused, then spoke

slowly and deliberately as if weighing each word. "Did you notice anything odd about the house next to yours?"

"Yes," I said. "There was a horse in the field last night, but it was barely moving. I think I saw it staring at us through the window last night. It was kind of creepy."

"*Creepy*. That horse is *way* more than creepy," Chris said.

"Why?"

"Because there is no horse," Chris said. "Well, that's not exactly right. There *used* to be a horse there."

"Used to be?" Sophie asked.

"Fifteen or twenty years ago," Nick said. "Real tall and black as night."

"What happened to it?" I asked. "Did the owners move or something?"

"No," Chris said. "It died."

CHAPTER 3

SOPHIE TOOK A SIP OF hot chocolate and, with a choc-olate moustache coating her upper lip, declared, "Needs more marshmallows."

We were sitting in Nick and Chris's kitchen, slowly warming up. My cheeks throbbed, and my fingers and toes tingled. We'd only taken our sleds down the hill a few more times before heading back.

"Help yourself," Nick said, sliding a yellow bag of mini marshmallows across the table to my sister.

Sophie drank half of her hot chocolate to free up some space in the mug, then dumped nearly a dozen marshmallows in. Mr. and Mrs. Russo, Nick and Chris's parents, were out, so there weren't any grown-ups around to tell us not to eat too much junk.

"So how do you guys know the horse died years ago if you've only been here five months?" I asked.

"All the kids talk about it at school," Chris said. "Most think it's just an old, nearly dead horse, but some people think it's a ghost. I even heard one kid say it was a zombie because there's no such thing as ghost horses. It's like a local legend."

"How did the horse die?" Sophie asked. "According to the legend."

"I've heard a few different stories," Nick said. "Some people say the horse died in a fire, which can't be true because the stable is still there, and it looks pretty old. Others say the family that lives in the house went bankrupt and chopped the horse up into bits and sold it for glue."

"That's also ridiculous," Chris said. "They don't use horses to make glue. Do they?"

Sophie nodded glumly. Chris looked shocked, then queasy. Then he shrugged it off and shoved a handful of marshmallows in his mouth.

Nick continued. "The story most people believe is that a couple of kids, two brothers, waited for nightfall then led the horse out of the stable and took it for a joyride into the woods behind the school. Then, when they were done with it..." Nick paused and ran his thumb across his throat.

"They killed the horse? Why?" Sophie said.

Nick shrugged.

"What happened to the brothers?" I asked, my throat dry. I took a sip of hot chocolate, but it didn't help.

"I don't know if I should tell you," Nick said.

"Come on, you can't just leave us hanging," I said.

"Well, I'll spare you the graphic details, but they were found dead in their beds one morning. Their bodies had been trampled as if by a horse."

"You didn't tell them the best part!" Chris said excitedly.

I didn't know how there was a "best part" of this story, but Chris was only too happy to fill us in. "The kids lived in an old house that was torn down before this subdivision was built, and their house was next door to the farmhouse with the horse. Right where you live now!"

As I had expected, I failed to see how that was the best part of the story. And judging by the look on my sister's face, so did she. But the rational side of me remembered that it was just a story. It was probably a big exaggeration or even totally made up. And even if it was true, what did it matter?

I loved fantasy and horror movies, but I didn't actually believe in ghosts. Real life wasn't like that. There was no such thing as a poltergeist.

Ouija boards were just a toy. And a ghost horse? Please.

Whoever lived in Briar Patch Farm had probably replaced the horse, that's all. As far as I was concerned, that was the most likely story, and I was happy to leave it at that.

⌒⊃⊂⌒

After we had finished our hot chocolate, we played a few games of *Kill Screen*, a game that was impossible to beat. Surprise, surprise—we didn't beat it. Not even close. Nick and I exchanged phone numbers before Sophie and I left. It was nearly lunchtime, and although Mom and Dad had said we didn't need to help, I felt like we should at least check in to see how things were going. Sophie wanted to stay a little longer, but I said Dad would probably make her favorite lunch: grilled cheese sandwiches and chicken noodle soup.

The moving truck had arrived, and a couple of guys were carrying our furniture into the house through the garage. Sophie and I crossed the street together, she a few steps behind me.

"That stuff they said about the kids being trampled to death by a horse was a little far-fetched," I said. "But let's stay away from that farmhouse—the horse, too—until we know a little more. Okay?"

Sophie didn't answer. I turned around. Sophie was gone.

"Sophie?" I called out.

The wind shrieked in response.

I turned toward the Russos' house. Sophie wasn't there. I looked up and down the street. I didn't see Sophie on the road or sidewalk. I was getting a little worried. Then, I finally spotted her.

She was standing on the front porch of the farmhouse.

"Sophie? What are you doing?"

She didn't answer. She put her hands up to a window and peered inside.

I ran down the sidewalk.

Sophie approached the front door. I sped up the porch steps.

Sophie raised her hand.

I grabbed her shoulder to stop her from doing what she was about to do, but I was too late.

Sophie knocked.

CHAPTER 4

KNOCK, KNOCK, KNOCK.

"Sophie," I whispered urgently. "Have you lost your mind? What are you doing?"

"There's no doorbell."

"That's not what I mean and you know it."

"I don't like mysteries," she said. "I want to know who lives here, I want to know what happened, and I want to know if they have a horse. A *living* horse."

I looked frantically from the door to the window. I didn't hear any sounds of approaching footsteps or see any movement in the window.

"It doesn't look like anyone's here," I said. "Let's go."

Sophie took a few steps back and gazed at the house. I joined her. She pointed at a window on the upper floor. The window's wooden slats were slightly open.

"I think that window was closed before," Sophie said. "Did you see?"

"No, now let's *go*." I tugged on Sophie's elbow but suddenly froze.

Something in the window had moved. Just a flash—there and gone.

I blinked and rubbed my eyes. "I must be seeing things. I thought I saw something in the window."

Sophie's face was pale and tense. "I saw it, too," she said quietly.

We shared a nervous glance and then, without saying another word, we turned and ran down the steps, along the sidewalk, and into the front hall of our house.

"Matt? Sophie? What's going on down there?" Mom shouted from the second floor. She peered over the railing. "You two look like you've seen a ghost."

Sophie and I looked at each other again. But this time we burst out laughing.

"Just playing, Mom," Sophie said. "We met a couple of kids from across the street, went sledding, drank hot chocolate, played video games, and had a race back here."

I raised my eyebrow at Sophie to say, *Not telling Mom about what just happened next door?*

She shrugged as if to say, *No way.*

I couldn't blame her—we hadn't really seen anything, anyway—so I faced Mom and nodded with a reassuring smile.

Mom seemed to have other things on her

mind. "All right. Well, these boxes aren't going to unpack themselves." She turned and disappeared.

"Wait!" Sophie shouted. "What about lunch?" Mom answered from one of the bedrooms.

"Your father made grilled cheese sandwiches and soup. Leftovers are in the refrigerator."

"Told ya." I smiled.

We took off our winter gear and weaved around randomly stacked boxes on our way to the kitchen. I took the food out of the fridge and put it in the microwave.

Sophie sat at the table. "Why were you such a chicken back there?"

I stopped what I was doing and stared at her. "That's private property. You were trespassing."

"It's not against the law to knock on a neighbor's door to introduce yourself."

"But that's not all you had in mind, is it? If I hadn't pulled you away you would have tested the doorknob to see if it was unlocked."

"Maybe."

"Are you serious?"

"C'mon," Sophie said, raising her hands in exasperation. "You're not curious?"

I was as curious as she was—maybe more so. "That's not the point. The point is...is—"

"WWBD?" Sophie interrupted, pointing at my T-shirt: WHAT WOULD BATMAN DO?

"Batman," I said with an air of geek superiority that I hoped would win me the argument, "is a superhero, one of the good guys. He would never break into someone's house."

"Batman wouldn't break into the Joker's lair to prevent him from doing something evil?"

"Yeah, I guess he probably would, but *A*," I held up fingers as I made my points, "we don't live next to the Joker; *B*, our neighbors aren't doing anything 'evil;' and C, we don't even know who lives there yet!" The microwave beeped. I turned back to it and tested the soup with my finger, then heated it up a little more.

Sophie sighed and looked out the kitchen window. "Still snowing...but no horse tracks in the field."

"What's your point?" I asked over my shoulder.

"Horses need lots of exercise, Matt," Sophie said in a huff.

"Okay, okay." I took the soup out of the micro-wave, then carried everything over to the table. "Something seems a little weird, I'll give you that. I still get goose bumps when I think of the horse staring in at us while we were eating pizza."

"That was late," Sophie said with a mouth full of grilled cheese. "Who would leave their horse out in the dark? That's just reckless."

I slurped a spoonful of hot soup and shrugged. "Who knows? Maybe we do live next to the Joker."

∽ට⊙෴

Later that night, long after my family had all gone to bed, and I'd read a few chapters of the latest Screamers book, I riffled through my box of Batman comics looking for one in particular. My conversation in the kitchen with Sophie had reminded me of a comic. I found it and flipped through its pages.

In the comic, Batman fights a villain called Gentleman Ghost, a phantom who wears a cape, a top hat, and a monocle. His main power is hurting living people with something he calls a "death touch." As far as Batman villains go, I always thought Gentleman Ghost wasn't very cool, but his horse was pretty awesome.

Gentleman Ghost rode a phantom horse, a giant white beast with glowing red eyes. The comic horse and the horse next door were both tall, but Gentleman Ghost's horse looked strong and healthy. The neighbors' horse looked ill and neglected.

I decided to show Sophie the Batman comic, assuming she hadn't fallen asleep yet. I crept down the hall, careful not to wake Mom and Dad, and opened her door.

"Sophie?" I whispered in the darkness. "You asleep?"

I expected to hear something along the lines of, *Not anymore, thanks to you.* But instead I was met with dead silence. I couldn't even hear her breathing.

My fingers fumbled up and down the wall until they landed on the light switch. I flicked it on. I immediately wished I could turn the light back off, turn back time, unsee what I had seen.

Sophie was lying in a bloody puddle in her bed.

Her body had been trampled and mangled.

CHAPTER 5

I RAN TO SOPHIE'S BEDSIDE. But as soon as I got there I stopped in confusion.

The gruesome image I had seen had disappeared. Not only was Sophie's bed no longer covered in blood, but Sophie wasn't lying in it at all. She was gone.

I closed and rubbed my eyes and was relieved that her bed was still empty when I looked again. Luckily I hadn't screamed, or else Mom and Dad would've rushed in, and then I'd have to explain why I'd been so scared. I didn't want to have that conversation.

"What is going on?" I whispered to myself. I'd never hallucinated before, and I'd definitely never imagined anything so disturbing. I made a mental note to cut back on Screamers books at bedtime and scanned the room for any sign of Sophie.

In addition to her bed, the movers had brought up her dresser, desk, and chair. There were a few stacks of unpacked boxes pushed up against one of the boring white walls. I didn't see anything that gave me any clues.

If I'd been out of bed at this time of night I'd have been watching TV, playing video games, or eating junk food. Sophie wasn't into movies and gaming as much as I was, so it had to be food. I turned off the bedroom light and snuck down to the kitchen.

Outside, the moon was blocked by clouds and the kitchen was nearly pitch-black. I turned on the light expecting to see my sister sitting at the table with a plate of food in front of her. She wasn't there, but at least I wasn't met with another gory hallucination.

Where was she?

There was a plate on the kitchen counter. I walked over for a closer look. On the plate was a small kitchen knife, sticky with juice, and an apple core. I assumed she'd eaten the apple, but it wasn't like Sophie to leave her dishes out.

My heart began to beat a little faster, and my palms grew sweaty. I had a bad feeling that something awful had happened to her. It was time to get Mom and Dad. They'd know what to do.

I turned off the kitchen light and started to head back upstairs, but then I noticed that the backyard light was on. That was odd. I looked out the window above the kitchen sink.

Something was out there—between my house and the farmhouse—something I'd seen before. Two large reflections of light.

Red eyes.

My vision adapted to the darkness, and soon I could make out the outline of the horse. It was approaching the fence.

I forgot about Sophie for a moment, as I wondered why the horse was out so late again. And then I thought of the two kids Nick and Chris had told us about, the two they claimed the horse had killed where my new house had been built.

That's when it clicked; and I realized why I had seen Sophie's battered body in her bed. It wasn't Screamers or the subconscious influence of anything else I'd read or watched lately. It had been planted in my mind by the story the brothers had told me earlier in the day. It was messing with my mind, making me see things. That was all.

The clouds parted in the sky, and the moon peeked out, full and bright. I could clearly see the horse, large and powerful. And now, in the silver-blue light of the moon and the snow, I could see what the horse was approaching.

Sophie. She was outside. What was she doing outside?

She had hopped over the log fence that separated our property from the farmhouse and was walking toward the horse. She reached out her hand. Her lips formed words but I couldn't hear her through the kitchen window.

The horse stopped when they were face-to-face and watched my sister for a tense moment. It bowed its head and sniffed at something in Sophie's hand.

Apple slices.

The horse snorted and pulled its head back.

I ran to the sliding glass door, opened it. I stuck my head out and was about to shout at Sophie to get back inside, but I froze, unable to make a sound. Someone had stepped out of the farmhouse. An old man. He looked furious. He pointed a pitchfork at Sophie and yelled, "Get away from my horse!"

Startled, Sophie dropped the apple slices.

The old man ran across the field with murder in his eyes.

And then the clouds covered the moon again. I could barely see a thing.

CHAPTER 6

WWBD?

He'd run straight outside, reach into his utility belt, knock out the old man with a well-thrown Batarang, jump onto the horse's back, and ride it to the stable where he'd lock it safely away.

I didn't have a utility belt loaded with gadgets nor the ability to jump up onto a horse's back, but I couldn't just stand in the kitchen and watch Sophie get attacked. I ran outside without even stopping to put on boots. The snow was so cold it felt like it burned the soles of my feet with every step.

"Sophie, move!" I yelled.

She didn't move. It was as if she didn't even hear me.

The old man was only about fifteen feet away from Sophie. He'd reach her in no time. He raised his pitchfork above his head.

I shouted again, louder this time. "Sophie, run!"

My words finally got through to Sophie. She broke out of her trance and started to run, but the man was still gaining on her. The sharp tips of his pitchfork were nearly within striking distance of my sister's back.

There was no time to lose. I picked up a large chunk of ice. It wasn't the best weapon in the world, but it was the best I could do.

"Sophie!" I shouted. "Get down!"

She looked at me, then the ice, then dropped to the ground.

I threw the ice at the old man like a shot put. Unlike Sophie, he didn't drop to the ground. He didn't need to. The ice sailed well over him and shattered on the ground.

But it slowed him down as he watched it pass.

Sophie joined me and we ran back to the house. I looked back once just before entering the kitchen.

The old man had given up the chase and was standing beside the horse on the other side of the fence. His hands tightened around the pitchfork as if he was trying to strangle it.

"Don't you ever cross this fence again, you hear me?" he warned us. He spoke calmly and quietly, and that scared me more than if he'd screamed and yelled. "Next time you come anywhere near Shade," he pointed at the horse, "I'll kill you both."

CHAPTER 7

AFTER CLOSING THE DOOR AND double-, triple-, quadruple-checking that it was locked, I took Sophie's hand and led her to the basement. We needed to talk, and I didn't want our parents to overhear us. She followed me as if in a daze.

I was surprised to find the basement already organized. IKEA bookshelves were filled with paperbacks, and storage stuff was neatly arranged on a row of metal shelves. Mom had been busier than I thought.

We sat side by side on an old couch. Sophie pulled her knees to her chest and hugged them. Her body shook. I gently rubbed her back, trying to calm her down.

"It's okay," I said in my most reassuring, soothing tone. "Everything is going to be all right."

I hoped that was true.

But after what had just happened—after the old man's threat—I wasn't so sure.

"Who was that guy?" Sophie said with a tremor in her voice.

"Our new neighbor, I guess."

"But why was he so angry? I didn't do anything wrong. I just wanted to give his horse an apple."

"I know," I said. "I know."

"I've never seen a horse turn down an apple before, but Shade took one sniff and turned up his nose. Did you notice that?"

I nodded.

"That's why I tried to feed him, to prove that the urban legend Nick and Chris told us is false, but...is it possible that Shade actually *is* a ghost?"

"I can't believe I'm going to say this, but yes, I do think it's possible," I said. "The weird thing is, the old man didn't seem to know that. If the horse—Shade—is a ghost, why would he feel the need to protect something that's already dead?"

"And why was he ready to stab me with his pitchfork just for jumping the fence?"

"If a couple of kids killed the horse, I guess the owner would be pretty distrustful of us."

"So what do we do now? What happens if he attacks us again?"

"We could go to the cops," I suggested.

"I don't know," Sophie said. "Could I get in trouble for trespassing?"

"We could tell Mom and Dad."

"Then I'd definitely get in trouble for trespassing." Sophie sighed. She was upset and not thinking rationally. "If I could just tell him why

I snuck over there—explain that I didn't want to hurt his horse—maybe he'd understand. Do you think?"

I shrugged and thought about it. It was doubtful, but Sophie was giving me a hopeful look, wishing I could magically make everything better. I didn't want to say no...

"I guess that might work," I said. "Mom always says an apology is the superglue of life—it can repair just about anything."

"I know!" Sophie said, perking up a little. "We could bake some cookies and take them over, kind of like a peace offering."

It seemed a little naive, but it was good to see my sister beginning to bounce back from the scare she'd just had. "When you say we can make cookies, you mean store-bought cookie dough, right?"

"Yeah, of course. Who doesn't like those?"

"No one, that's who," I said.

Sophie nodded and even laughed a little. "I

feel a little better already. Just do me a favor and don't tell Mom and Dad, at least not yet. They'll never let me out of the house again. I'll be grounded forever."

"All right, but if the neighbor freaks out and doesn't accept your apology, I'll have to tell them."

"Deal?"

"Deal."

Clunk!

We jumped and yelped in unison. One of Sophie's old dolls had fallen off a shelf and landed on the floor. The doll wore a pink dress and had short brown hair. Her name was Sadie Sees. Sophie loved the name Sadie because it was so close to her own.

I was about to say how creepy it had been that the doll had fallen but was interrupted by Sadie herself.

"Wouldn't it be fun," the doll said in a high-pitched, warbling voice, *"if you were a doll like*

me?" When Sadie spoke, her oversized eyes rolled around in their sockets and her tiny mouth opened and closed out of time with her words.

Neither Sophie nor I moved for nearly a minute.

We sat frozen and stared at Sadie.

"How did it fall off the shelf?" I asked without taking my eyes off the doll.

Sophie shook her head slowly. "I don't know. I didn't see."

We looked at each other one more time, then sprinted up the stairs.

CHAPTER 8

THAT NIGHT I DREAMT OF Sadie Sees's headless body riding a giant black horse through the woods, like Ichabod Crane in "The Legend of Sleepy Hollow." But even without a head, Sadie could still talk.

Wouldn't it be fun if you were a doll like me?

I wish you and I were twins.

I can see through anything.

My imagination was clearly getting the better of me.

When I woke up, I rubbed my eyes, took a deep breath, and forced all thought of Sadie out of my mind.

"Matt! Sophie! Breakfast is on the table, and it's not getting any warmer!" It was Dad, calling up from the main floor.

I pulled on a pair of jeans and a fresh T-shirt with a picture of the Millennium Falcon on it, then made my way downstairs. I was surprised to find that I had beat my sister down to the kitchen. She was an early riser, while I tended to stay up late and sleep in.

"Morning, champ," Dad said as he set a plate in front of me. After yesterday's Cheerios, he'd really upped his game. Scrambled eggs, two strips of bacon, a pile of hash browns, and two pieces of white toast. One piece of toast had Darth Vader's helmet toasted on it, while the other piece had the Star Wars logo. He'd obviously used the toaster Mom had bought him for Christmas. That wasn't surprising, since it's the only toaster he'd used since then. "Appropriate shirt," Dad said, pointing at my shirt, then at the toast.

Sophie stumbled into the kitchen like an extra from a zombie movie. She sat heavily on the chair across from me and barely had the energy to keep her head off the table.

"Rough night?" Mom asked Sophie.

"Ungh," Sophie muttered.

"It might take a couple of days before we're used to sleeping in our new rooms," I offered, covering for Sophie since she didn't seem capable of forming words, let alone thoughts, on her own.

Dad placed a plate in front of my sister. She latched on to a strip of bacon, raised it to her mouth, and chewed it slowly, like a cow munching on grass.

"So," Mom said, "any big plans for the day? Going to head out exploring again?"

Sophie continued to eat her bacon. She stared at the table. She didn't appear to be aware of the rest of us.

"Yeah, kind of," I said. "The guys across the street invited us over again, and we thought we should take some cookies or something." I didn't like lying to my parents, but I knew that if I said we were going to introduce ourselves to the farm-house neighbors, Mom and Dad would want to meet them, too. And then they'd find out about last night's confrontation. And that couldn't happen, at least not yet. "Do we have some cookie dough?"

Mom tsked and took her plate to the sink. "No self-respecting child of mine is going to offer pre-made cookies to our new neighbors. That might be good enough for us, but not for new friends. I'll help you bake cookies from scratch."

"Mom?" I said as gently as possible. "You don't bake. Or cook. You don't even make toast."

"That's only because your father won't let me touch his Darth Vader toaster. And I'll have you know that I used to be a great cook when I first met your father and had more time. Wasn't I, dear?"

Dad looked at me and smiled. "She made a mean Kraft Dinner."

"You better believe it!" Mom said. "My secret ingredient was pepper." She zipped around the kitchen, opening and closing cupboards at random. "Now, where are the cookbooks?"

"Still packed," Dad said.

Mom started a search on her phone. "No matter. Chef Google will help us out. Ah! Here we go. A recipe for Mom's Famous Chocolate Chip Cookies. Sounds perfect." She scrolled through whatever website she had landed on and mumbled to herself as she read. "Ingredients... do we have...instructions...wow, seven steps... remove hot baking sheet from oven, that sounds dangerous..."

"Sweetheart?" Dad said kindly.

"Mm-hmm?"

"I'll help."

"Thank you."

"No problem." Dad pointed at his apron. "After all, we have cookies."

Mom smiled. I laughed. Sophie groaned.

Sophie and I stood at the end of our driveway. She had slowly come back to life while eating her breakfast and, with Dad's help, the cookies hadn't taken long to bake. We had placed them in an old tin and had set out soon after. Mom and Dad were returning to housework, so they probably—hopefully—wouldn't see us head next door instead of across the street.

"Are you sure we should do this?" Sophie asked. "The old man was really angry. He threatened to kill us. Maybe we should just pretend it didn't happen and avoid him and his horse from now on, like he said."

I shook my head and zipped up my jacket

against the wind. "We need to go talk to him now or else things will get really awkward. It's not like he lives down the street or around the corner—he lives next door. We're going to see him a lot, and things got blown out of proportion. You were just trying to feed the horse some apple slices, but maybe he thought you were trying to, I don't know, hurt it or something. I'm sure once we explain that your intentions were good, he'll understand. Plus, he's probably calmed down overnight."

Sophie didn't look 100 percent convinced, but nodded and followed as I walked to the front porch. I handed her the tin of cookies.

"Why are you giving these to me?" she asked.

"You're the one who got us in this mess. You give him the cookies." She sighed.

I knocked on the door.

"Remember," I whispered sideways to my sister, "be remorseful."

"Why?" she whispered back.

"You want him to know you feel guilty."

"I don't feel guilty," Sophie said, her tone rising. "I didn't do anything wrong!"

"Keep it down," I said, my whisper beginning to rise in volume. "And remember we're here to make things better, not worse. *Be remorseful.*"

"*You* be remorseful!"

"That doesn't make any sense."

Sophie shoved the cookie tin back into my hands and threw her arms in the air. "That's it! Forget this. I'm leaving." She turned to storm off.

"Wait! Did you hear that?"

Sophie shook her head.

"It sounded like wood clacking against wood." I pointed up. "From above."

We took a few steps back and looked up at the second-floor window. The same one in which we thought we'd seen movement the day before.

Someone with fiery eyes and ashen skin was peering down at us.

CHAPTER 9

IT WASN'T THE MAN FROM the night before.

It was an old woman. She looked at us with an expression so odd that I couldn't tell if she was surprised, angry, or merely curious. It felt weird to stand there and stare up as she stared down—no one moving, no one talking—so I raised a hand and waved.

She receded into the darkness without waving back.

"I don't like this," Sophie said. "I want to go."

"Where?" I asked.

"Anywhere but here."

"It's fine. She's probably on her way down to answer the door."

Sophie shook her head. "I've got a bad feeling about this. I've got a bad feeling about *her*."

"She's just an old woman. We have nothing to be afraid of." My voice caught in my throat as I said the word *nothing*.

"I'm leaving," Sophie said, but she didn't get the chance.

The door opened.

Just a crack. Long, bony fingers slipped out of the house and gripped the edge of the door, holding it in place as if whoever was inside was afraid the wind might blow it open. As if whoever was inside was hiding something.

"Who are you and what do you want?" It was a scratchy and frail voice, as if she hadn't spoken in many years.

I cleared my throat and stepped back onto the

porch. "My name is Matt, ma'am, and this is my sister Sophie. We just moved in next door and, well, we brought you some cookies."

"They're homemade," Sophie added, following me reluctantly.

I held up the tin.

There was no response at first, but then the door creaked open a little wider. The woman stuck her head and neck outside to get a better look at us. Her beady, sunken eyes moved from me to Sophie to the tin.

"Open that up," she said.

I popped the lid off the tin and showed her the contents: Mom's Famous Chocolate Chip Cookies, made with love by Dad. And us. And although Mom didn't end up doing any of the baking, she Googled the recipe, so I guess she should get a little credit, too.

The woman reached a shaking hand into the tin and pulled out one of the smaller cookies. She raised the cookie to her open mouth, but before she took a bite, she paused, then looked at me and my sister. Then, stranger still, she held it out to me.

"You eat it," she said with a sinister grin.

"What?"

"I said, you eat it. I can't accept food from a stranger. What if it's poisoned?"

"It's not—"

"If there's nothing wrong with it," the woman said, interrupting me, "you have nothing to fear."

I looked at Sophie then shrugged, accepted the cookie, took a big bite, chewed, and swallowed. "See? They're fine."

After a sharp nod, the woman took the tin and quickly ate two cookies before putting the lid back on. I couldn't believe how quickly she'd eaten them, like a ravenous bear coming out of hibernation and finding a bloody deer carcass.

"Thank you," she said with a hint of shame. She wiped cookie crumbs off her lips and frowned. "Why did you bring these?"

"Like I said before, we just moved—"

She interrupted me again. "The real reason. You don't expect me to believe a couple of kids decided to bake cookies for their elderly neighbor who they've never met, do you?"

I sighed. "All right, you got us. We brought them over as an apology."

I paused and looked at Sophie, and when she didn't say anything I elbowed her.

"I'm sorry!" she shouted, snapping out of her catatonic state.

"For what?" the woman said.

"I, um, snuck into your backyard last night," Sophie said. "I just wanted to give your horse some apple slices."

I wanted to keep things upbeat so I added, "Sophie loves horses, and she really likes Shade. He's a beautiful animal."

"You saw Shade? How do you know his name? Who have you spoken to?"

Her rapid-fire questions caught me by surprise.

I didn't know how to respond.

"Your husband told us his name," Sophie said.

"My husband?"

Sophie nodded and looked at the ground. "Yeah, he ran outside and chased us off. He said... Well, he told us to stay away from the horse."

He told us he'd kill us if we went anywhere near Shade again, I thought, but Sophie was smart to leave that unsaid. It wouldn't have done any good.

Even though Sophie had softened the story somewhat, the woman looked taken aback. She cupped her cheek with a hand and looked at her reflection in the door's small glass window. "My husband," she said. "Yes, of course. I heard him run outside last night. I guess that's when he chased you."

"He hasn't mentioned what happened last night at all today?" I asked. That was a little weird. You'd think he would've talked about it with his wife by then.

When I saw the look on the woman's face I realized I shouldn't have asked such a personal question. Her mouth was open a crack, and her eyes bored into my own as if she was trying to mine my soul.

"No, he hasn't," she said. "He's...not here. I don't see him during the day."

At all? Ever? I wondered, but at least this time I had the good sense to keep my thoughts to myself. Sophie reached into her pocket and pulled out her phone. "Sorry," she said as she held the phone out in front of her face and typed on the screen. "I got a text from Mom." She put her phone away and looked at me. "We have to go. She wants to see us."

"What did she say?" I asked.

Sophie shrugged and turned to the woman. She gave her a quick smile. "Sorry again about your horse." Then, turning back to me, added, "C'mon."

Sophie was acting weird. I could tell something

was wrong. Mom must have been really mad at us, but I had no idea what we had done. Maybe she saw us come over here instead of going across the street.

"Enjoy the cookies," I said, only then realizing the woman hadn't introduced herself. "Mrs....?"

"Thank you," she said, dodging my question and giving Sophie an odd, quizzical look. She shut the front door with a slam.

"Well, that didn't go as well as I had hoped," I said, staring at the closed door.

"Quick, let's go," Sophie said. She rushed back to our house, but when we got there she didn't go inside. Instead, she led me to the narrow space between our house and the new one on the other side.

"I thought Mom—" I started, but Sophie raised her hand and cut me off.

"You know how the woman said she never sees her husband during the day? That he wasn't there?" she asked.

Sophie's face was pale, and she was breathing fast.

"Yeah," I said.

"Then how do you explain this?" She held out her phone.

I took it from her and looked at the screen.

Sophie had taken a picture just moments before while we stood on the farmhouse porch. I could see the open door, the woman and behind her, peering out from the shadows of the hallway with a look of hatred, was the old man.

CHAPTER 10

IT WAS DEFINITELY THE OLD man who had rushed out of the house the night before, but he looked a little different in the picture than he had in the flesh.

His skin looked much paler—so pale, in fact, that it seemed to give off a faint glow. A white ring of light like a lens flare encircled his head. Only his face could be seen. It appeared to float in the darkness as if he didn't have a body. His shoulders, chest, and limbs were concealed by shadow. And although the photo was in focus, the old man's face was blurry, softening his facial features and making his eyes look like two small charcoal smudges.

I handed the phone back to Sophie. "You took this when you said Mom texted you?"

Sophie nodded. "He appeared right after I told his wife that he chased us off. At first I thought my eyes were playing tricks on me, since all I could see was his face, but he didn't go away. He kept on watching us. So I pretended I got a text and took a picture instead."

I was impressed. I hadn't looked inside and down the hall—I'd been focused on the woman, trying to figure out what it was about her that made me feel suspicious of her. "So the woman was lying about him being out and about never seeing him during the day. I wonder what else she lied about?"

"She gave me a weird feeling. She was definitely hiding something."

"I think so, too. How didn't she hear her

husband run out of the house last night? Actually, she seemed shady about their whole relationship. When you first mentioned him she didn't seem to know who you were talking about."

"Yeah, you're right. And she didn't want to tell us her name. I wonder why?"

"I do, too," I said. A cold current of air howled between the houses and stung my face and hands. "And I can think of two people who might be able to help us."

Luckily, the Russo brothers were home, bored and only too happy to talk to us about our creepy neighbors.

Chris answered the door and led us to the family room, where Nick was watching an episode of *Screamers*, the show based on the books. It was the one where Zoë Winter, one of the recurring actors on the show, was playing a girl who thought she was admitted to a modern hospital, only to discover late in the episode that she's suffering from hallucinations and the hospital is not only abandoned, but haunted.

"I love this episode," I said, sitting down on the couch and momentarily forgetting why we were there.

"Matt, we didn't come over to watch...whatever show this is," Sophie said.

I cringed at my sister's ignorance but nodded—she wasn't wrong—and turned to face Nick and Chris. "We just met the old woman who lives in the farmhouse, and, well... Sophie, why don't you just show them the picture?"

Sophie unlocked her phone, pulled up the picture, and handed it over to Nick. He looked at the screen and then passed it to his younger brother with a shrug and a blank look.

"Who's the old guy?" Chris asked.

"He lives in the house," Sophie said. "I think it's just him and his wife."

"Sophie took that picture while we were talking to her at the front door. She implied that he's never around during the day—I assumed she meant he works long hours or something— but then he appeared behind her in the shadows. You've never seen him before?"

"No, never," Nick said. "We've never seen anyone there. Literally not a soul. Just that horse."

"Shade," Sophie said. "Huh?"

"The horse's name is Shade."

"You had quite the long talk with the woman, didn't you?" said Nick.

"Well," Sophie said, drawing the word out like an elastic band, "that's not all we did. I maybe-kinda-sorta hopped the fence last night and tried to feed the horse."

"Are you kidding me?" Chris exclaimed with a look of shock painted across his face.

"Nope," Sophie said with a sheepish shrug.

"Epic," Nick said. "You're brave!"

Sophie's guilty look quickly transformed into one of pride.

"He looks freaky," Chris said. He couldn't take his eyes off Sophie's phone.

"He acts freaky, too," I said. "He totally lost it and threatened to kill us."

"Well, that lines up with the story of the kids who died on your property," Nick said. After seeing the uneasy look on my face, he added, "If you believe in the urban legend, that is."

I fidgeted in my seat and cleared my throat but didn't say anything.

"What are you thinking?" Sophie asked. She knew me well.

"It's weird," I said. "We've all seen the horse, but you two—" I pointed at Nick and Chris "—have never seen the people. That means they rarely leave the house, but horses need lots of attention. Right, Sophie?"

She nodded. "They need to be fed, brushed, they need exercise, medical care..."

I continued. "The old couple are shut-ins. You've never even seen them in the field or near the stable! So who's taking care of Shade? Unless, of course, Shade doesn't need to be taken care of. No food, no brushing, no nothing."

"Because Shade is the same horse that those kids killed in the woods behind the school," Nick said, nodding in agreement. "And he's come back for revenge."

"If that's true," Sophie said, "and that's a big if, because we're talking about a ghost horse and we live in the real world, not a fairy tale—the horse might have a grudge against all children. Or at least kids who live beside it."

"Maybe," I said. "Maybe not. But just to be safe, no more jumping over the fence, okay?"

Chris, who was still studying Sophie's phone as if there was going to be a quiz and he was trying to commit every detail to memory, opened his mouth to say something. But just then, a man walked into the family room. He looked like an older version of the boys. It was obviously Mr. Russo.

"Hey, kids," he said. "I didn't know you had friends over."

"Yeah, this is Matt and Sophie. They just moved in across the street," Nick said.

Mr. Russo grabbed Chris's shoulders and squeezed them in a fatherly way. He looked at the phone in his son's hand. His expression soured immediately. "Where'd you find that picture?"

"We didn't find it," Chris said. "Sophie took it this morning."

Their dad laughed in disbelief, a bitter sound that fought to reject what Chris had said. "She must be playing a prank on you. And frankly, it's not funny."

Sophie shook her head, her eyes wide and surprised. "I don't know what you're talking about."

"She really did take the picture this morning," I said, backing up my sister.

Mr. Russo crossed his arms and took on a stern

look. It was clear that he'd made up his mind, and he wasn't going to believe a word we said. "Impossible. That man—Ernest Creighton—and his wife used to live in the house beside yours." He paused, then added, "They both died more than twenty years ago."

CHAPTER 11

NEEDLESS TO SAY, A STUNNED silence filled the Russos' family room.

We'd been so focused on the possibility of Shade being a ghost that we hadn't stopped to consider that the old couple were ghosts, too. But now that I thought about it, I couldn't believe I'd missed the warning signs. They both looked dead—Mr. Creighton's pale, glowing skin, and his wife's thinness.

I asked Mr. Russo how he recognized Ernest Creighton, since he'd died so long ago.

"I grew up in Courtice, in a house not too far from here. My friends and I all thought Briar Patch Farm was a creepy place back then, same as kids think now. There was an obituary in the local paper when Mr. Creighton died—said he died of a heart attack or something. But rumors quickly spread that there'd been some sort of foul play involved."

"What sort of foul play?" I asked.

"Don't you worry about that. Like I said, it was just a rumor, kids trying to scare other kids. I guess times don't change much." He shook his head and left the room.

"I thought the old man looked like a ghost," Chris said. "I was just about to say so when Dad came in and saw the phone."

"Don't worry about our dad," Nick said. "We believe you. The question is, what do we do now?"

No one had any idea.

It was late and Sophie and I sat in our family room, talking in hushed tones. Our parents were in the other room.

"But she ate two cookies," Sophie said. "Ghosts don't eat, do they?"

I shrugged. "I don't know. I don't think so." I racked my brain for an answer. "Wait, Slimer eats. A lot."

"Who's Slimer?"

"*Ghostbusters*. Round green guy with no legs."

"Oh yeah, right." Sophie scrunched up her face.

"He's not exactly realistic though, is he?"

"Before today, would you have said a ghost horse is realistic? Or ghosts at all, for that matter?"

"Good point." Sophie looked out the window at the farmhouse. There wasn't a cloud in the sky, and the moonlight reflected brightly off the snow, making the world glow. "So, what do we do now? Do we tell Mom and Dad?"

"They wouldn't believe us. Plus, we told them we were going across the street this morning, remember? I don't think they'd be too happy to find out we lied to them."

"Then what?"

"I think the best thing to do is avoid the Creightons' house for a while. Scratch that: forever. If we don't bug them, maybe they won't bug us. And hopefully they're, like, tied to their house or something, and can't wander off the property. Ernest didn't chase us over the fence last night."

Sophie nodded but then frowned and pursed her lips. "But the story claims they came over here and killed the two kids in their beds."

I sighed. "I didn't think of that."

"What are you two talking about?"

My stomach dropped. It was Mom, standing in the doorway to the family room. I didn't know how much she'd overheard.

Neither Sophie nor I could think of an appropriate response.

"Kids being killed in their beds?" Mom said. She looked from me to Sophie. "Has he gotten you into those horror books and movies he likes?"

"Oh, yeah," Sophie said. "A little, I guess. We watched an episode of, um, *Shivers* earlier today."

Luckily Mom wasn't too familiar with horror—if it had been Dad, he would have known the show was called *Screamers*, and we would've been busted for sure.

Mom pointed at Sophie. "Well, if you have nightmares tonight, you're too big to sleep in my bed. You're on your own."

I breathed a sigh of relief.

<hr />

Later that night, after we'd put on our pajamas, brushed our teeth, gone to our separate rooms, turned off our bedroom lights, and waited to hear the telltale snores coming from Mom and Dad's room, Sophie snuck into my room. We'd decided to meet once our parents were asleep. I had something I wanted to show Sophie.

After Sophie quietly shut my door, I turned on the bedside lamp. She looked dejected.

"What's the matter?" I asked, expecting her to be scared or upset at the thought of living next door to a couple of dead people and their dead horse.

"I have to watch horror movies with you now," she said, "and read horror books, or else Mom will get suspicious."

I laughed quietly. "Come on, they're not that bad. You might actually like them."

She shook her head. "I didn't like them before all this, and now... Now I'm living in a horror story."

"You know Mom; her head's always so full of numbers and lists that she'll probably forget all about what you said in a day or two."

"I hope so." Sophie sighed. "What did you want to show me?"

I handed her the Batman comic book I had found the night before. Sophie sat on the bed beside me and gazed down at Gentleman Ghost in his cape, top hat, and monocle, riding on his phantom horse. "Does that horse look familiar?"

"It looks just like Shade," Sophie said. "But white and a bit more healthy. And, um, glowy."

"My thoughts exactly."

"Why are you showing it to me? It's just a comic."

"WWBD? Maybe there's something in the story line that could help us deal with Shade and the Creightons. Some clue or something."

"I didn't think we were going to go anywhere near them again."

"Well, yeah, that's the best plan. But what if they're able to come over here? What if they can enter our house? What if they actually did kill those kids?" I was about to add *We need to be prepared*, when I was interrupted by the sound of something falling.

Sophie and I spun around and stared at the source of the sound. It had come from inside my closet.

"What was that?" Sophie whispered urgently.

The door was closed, so we couldn't see inside.

I shook my head and shrugged, unable to answer. In the stillness that followed, my skin began to crawl.

"Do you hear that?" Sophie said, her panic rising.

I nodded. From behind the closet door, I could definitely hear whispering.

CHAPTER 12

THE WHISPERING SUDDENLY STOPPED, AS if whoever was in the closet knew they had been heard.

Sophie and I stared at each other. We couldn't do anything other than breathe, and even that was proving to be a minor challenge. Long ago I had outgrown the fear that monsters were in my closet, but now one of my worst childhood nightmares appeared to be coming to life.

We waited.

Nothing happened. Nothing jumped out of the closet. There was no more noise from within.

I couldn't take the silence any longer.

"H-h-hello?" I said shakily. "Is there anyone in there?"

There was no answer.

Sophie looked at me like I was bananas. Like I shouldn't have made our presence known. But I was filled with curiosity, and I couldn't keep quiet.

"We know there's somebody in there. This is my room, so you better come out now, or else." Or else what, I had no idea. My focus was on trying to sound confident and strong, but I feared I had failed on both counts.

Maybe my command worked. Or maybe the things in my closet weren't intimidated by me at all. Whatever the case, the handle turned, the closet door creaked open, and something came out.

A hand—small, bony, and pale white. It gripped the edge of the door. The darkness of the closet obscured the person who had cracked open the door. I was consumed by two opposite but powerful forces: the desire to run out of the room and the paralyzing fear that rooted me to the floor. I looked at Sophie, and she seemed to have the same problem. Her eyes were wide, her mouth was drawn tight, and her head was drawn back as if she was trying to get as far away from the closet as possible.

And then the voice from the closet broke the silence with three words, repeated three times, that started as a quiet hiss and grew louder with each word.

"You're both dead, you're both dead, *you're both dead*."

"Who are you?" I blurted out. "What do you want with us?" I sounded desperate and terrified and I no longer cared. I *was* desperate and terrified.

"Stop scaring us and come out or go away," Sophie said. Her eyes were wet with tears, and her cheeks were flushed. Her clenched fists hit my bed when she said the word away.

The door creaked open a little more.

"I'm sorry," the voice said. "But if you're not scared, you should be."

That's when I noticed something odd about the hand. The fingernails were wet and the liquid was dark, almost black. The hand slid down the door five or six inches, smearing the wood—not black but red.

It was blood. My stomach flipped at the sight of it. Then I noticed something else. The fingers were oddly disjointed, as if every knuckle had been dislocated and every bone had been cracked.

Sophie gave me a *what do we do?* look. I shrugged.

"All right," the voice said. "I'll come out so we can...talk. But Jack will probably stay in the closet, if you don't mind. He's easily startled."

Jack? I thought. *Who's Jack? How many people are in my closet?*

I didn't know what to say, so I didn't say anything. Mom always said silence is golden, but I'm not sure this was what she had in mind.

After a brief, hesitant pause, the door opened all the way. A boy stepped out of the closet and into the light of my room.

To say that he didn't look good would be the understatement of my life.

CHAPTER 13

SOPHIE AND I JUMPED TO our feet and raced to the other side of the bed. My heart pounded in my ears with every painful beat, and I felt dizzy with fear and revulsion. Sophie opened her mouth to scream. I quickly covered her mouth with my hand and hugged her to me, partly to keep her quiet, partly to comfort myself. I'd never been so scared in my life.

The boy didn't walk out of the closet. At least, not in the way I or Sophie or the Russo brothers would have. He staggered out of the closet. Like a kid who still managed to walk despite having two broken knees. And ankles. And feet. He was dressed in pajamas, the pants bloody and his left pant leg torn. A jagged piece of shinbone protruded through the rip. I couldn't believe that he was standing, let alone walking.

It wasn't just his legs that were badly injured, but his arms, too. And like his pants, his shirt was soaked in blood.

Amazingly, the boy's face was unharmed. It wasn't even bruised. But his skin was pale white and dark circles hung beneath his eyes, making his sockets look larger than they were. Those eyes widened as he watched us from across the room, as if he'd just realized something. He looked down at his broken, bloodied body and then back at us.

"I'm sorry," he said. "I sometimes forget how I look. I haven't talked to anyone in...a long time. Well, other than Jack." He pointed back at my closet. And then I watched—half amazed, half horrified—this was the weirdest thing I'd ever seen, and that list was getting longer by the minute. The boy hunched over, raised his right hand in the air above his skull, and then slowly passed it down over his body from head to toe. His hand somehow healed all his wounds, erasing bruises and mending bones, but it did more than that—it even cleaned the blood off his skin and repaired his clothes. He stood up straight and tall, looking every inch like a brand-new boy.

"How did you do that?" I asked in a whisper.

He shrugged and looked at the ground as if he'd suddenly grown shy.

"You're one of the brothers who used to live here, aren't you?" Sophie asked, and I immediately knew she was right. It explained why he was here and why he'd been in such rough shape. Part of me had a hard time believing it, but it appeared as if the urban legend was true.

The boy nodded.

"What's your name?" Sophie asked. I was

impressed her voice was so even and calm. I couldn't talk at all at that moment.

"Daniel," he said. "Everyone calls me Danny."

"What happened to you?"

After a few false starts, Danny finally told us his story. He and his twin brother Jack had lived in an old country house that used to be on our land, as the Russos had said, and they had stolen Shade and ridden him late one night. But they hadn't slit Shade's throat. The horse had slipped on a sheet of ice at the top of the sledding hill and fallen awkwardly on one of his legs. The boys jumped off the horse as Shade rolled down the hill and crashed into the trunk of a thick maple tree. A loud crack split the air. Shade fell limp.

"But we didn't mean to kill the horse, I swear!" Danny said. "We just wanted to go for a quick ride. The Creightons were always so mean and never let us go anywhere near Shade. The fall... It was an accident."

I felt sorry for Danny and his brother. They

had done something they shouldn't have, but Danny clearly felt awful. I knew what that was like. I'd made plenty of mistakes that could've ended badly, but luckily hadn't. Bad things can happen to anyone.

His brother. The whispers we'd heard in the closet. I'd forgotten all about him. "Does Jack, um, want to come out now?"

Danny looked over his shoulder and into the darkness of the closet. He turned back to face us and shook his head.

"How did you..." Sophie started to ask before trailing off. She swallowed, then started again. "What happened next?"

Danny shook his head. It was as if the reality of the situation still hadn't sunk in after twenty years. "Two policemen came to the door the next day, but my parents had no clue we'd snuck out so they promised we'd been in bed all night. And I insisted that I hadn't ever gone near the horse. The police bought it, but Mr. Creighton was staring me down from his front porch. He knew. Somehow he knew."

Danny sighed and shifted his weight with a loud series of cracks and pops. Even though his body *looked* better, it still sounded broken.

"That evening, I woke up in the middle of the night. I'd dreamt that Mr. Creighton had snuck into my house, walked down the hall, and entered my room. When I opened my eyes, I realized it wasn't a dream, but it wasn't Mr. Creighton in my doorway. It was Shade. The horse stared me down as if he enjoyed seeing how scared I was. And then Shade had his revenge."

My imagination filled in the rest. The horse trampled Danny in his bed, his hooves pounding his small body.

"And after Shade killed you," Sophie said, "he killed your brother?"

Staring at the ground, Danny nodded. "Can we talk to him?" I asked.

"I already told you he's easily startled."

"Wait a minute," I said, thinking back to the night before. If Jack was easily startled... "Were you both in the basement last night listening to Sophie and me talking? Jack knocked a doll off the toy shelf, didn't he?"

Danny nodded. "Yeah. That was my brother."

I walked around the bed and headed toward the open closet. "He has nothing to fear, not from us. Jack? You can come out."

"No!" Danny roared. He jumped in front of me and blocked my path, a look of pure fury on his face. It caught me completely off guard, and for a moment I thought he was going to attack me. But then he turned and fled into the closet. The door slammed shut behind him.

Silence.

For the second time that night my heart pounded, and I felt like I might pass out. I sat on my bed and slowly began to feel a little better.

"Well, that was really weird," Sophie said.

"Yeah, no kidding."

Neither of us spoke for a moment, and then Sophie smiled slightly. "I guess this place isn't as boring as I thought it would be."

I laughed. It felt good, a relief, but if I gave it too much thought I knew the feeling was only surface deep. I wished we'd moved to a regular, run-of-the-mill, sleepy suburb, even though that had been the last thing I'd wanted a few days ago. Not only did we now live beside a haunted house, but we lived in a haunted house. Period. Full stop.

I had a feeling bad things were about to happen, and I had no idea how to prevent them.

CHAPTER 19

SOPHIE OFFERED TO LET ME sleep in her room for the night. I waved her off and told her I'd be fine. She left.

I closed my bedroom door and turned off the light. I ran across my room and jumped into bed, afraid something might reach out from beneath it and grab my foot. I hadn't done that since I was six years old.

I pulled my duvet up to my chin and stared at the ceiling, the wall, the window...anywhere but the closet. I closed my eyes, but all I could see was the horse crushing Sophie and me into a bloody pulp.

I opened my eyes.

I ran quietly down the hall to my sister's bedroom.

∽◦⊙◦∽

Light streamed in through Sophie's window the next morning and shined in my eyes. I sat up groggily, rubbed my face, yawned, and slowly took in my surroundings. I was on the floor next to Sophie's bed, a duvet balled up at my feet. Sophie was lying in her bed, her back to me.

I hadn't slept well, and my brain took a little longer than usual to warm up.

"Sophie," I whispered. "Wake up."

She rolled over immediately and faced me. "I've been awake for a while."

"Oh, okay. Listen, I think we should do a little digging, see what we can find out about Danny and the Creightons. It might help us deal with them both. Grab your phone."

She raised her phone in the air. "Way ahead of you, big brother. Check this out." She handed me her phone.

On the screen was a newspaper article from twenty-three years earlier. The headline read, "Parents of Slain Twin Brothers Main Suspects in Double Homicide."

I read the article to myself while my sister sat and watched me.

"Huh," I said.

"Yup," Sophie said.

"So the police thought their parents killed them since there was no sign of anyone else breaking into their house."

Sophie nodded gravely. "Ghosts don't need to break in, do they?"

"The parents must have been a mess. Not only did they lose both their kids, but they were blamed for the murders."

"If it makes you feel any better, I read another article that said they weren't convicted since there wasn't enough evidence against them."

"A little, I guess."

Sophie shrugged, then pointed at the phone still in my hand. "Swipe right and read the next article I found."

It was Mr. Creighton's obituary, published a week before the article about Danny and Jack. The main points jumped out at me as I raced to the end. He had died of a heart attack, and the article said he was to be buried beside his wife, Hazel, in a local cemetery. It was a short article that wasn't too revealing. Until, that is, I reached the final sentence.

I looked at Sophie, then back at her phone. I reread the sentence to myself, then read it again aloud.

"'Ernest is survived by his daughter, Clara.'"

"Yeah," Sophie said, taking her phone back. "Which kinda raises a question."

I nodded. "Where is Clara now?"

CHAPTER 15

I WAS RELIEVED WHEN THE doorbell rang that afternoon and I found Nick and Chris standing outside on our front porch.

"Hey, Matt," Nick said. "Want to go sledding?" Standing behind Nick, Chris raised his sled in the air as if I needed the visual cue to understand.

"Yes, yes, and yes," I said, not caring if I sounded too desperate. I was thankful for the distraction and thought it would be the perfect way to clear my head. "Let me go get Sophie."

The four of us were on the hill within ten minutes.

The air was cool and dry and burned my lungs with every breath. My nose and cheeks tingled as if on fire.

"Thanks for asking us to come," I said between breaths after climbing the hill for the third time.

"No problem," Nick said. "You seemed, uh, pretty enthusiastic."

"Yeah, I guess you could say that." I laughed to show that I wasn't embarrassed. "I was beginning to feel locked up."

"You've only been here three days," Nick pointed out dryly.

"What can I say? They've been three of the strangest days ever. And after your dad told us about Mr. Creighton and his wife being dead, even stranger things have happened."

"Oh, yeah?" Chris said. "Like what?"

"Um, we saw another ghost?" Sophie said,

sounding like she was unsure it had actually happened.

"Another ghost?" Chris asked loudly. "Wow!"

"*Shhh*," I said, looking over both shoulders, fearful that someone might be skulking in the bushes around us.

"Where?" Nick asked. "In the Creightons' house?"

"No. In..." I paused, still not overjoyed by the thought of having a dead roommate. "In my bedroom."

"IN YOUR—"

This time Sophie and Nick both joined me in shushing Chris. His winter-reddened cheeks reddened even deeper.

"In your bedroom?" he whispered.

I nodded. "And that's not all. His name is Danny, and the stories are true. He used to live in a house on our property, and he was killed by the ghost of Shade." I paused and frowned, unsure if the Russo brothers would believe the next bit, or if Chris would shout so loud his head would explode. "And Danny's twin, Jack, also kind of seems to be living in my closet. Well, not *living*, I guess, but...yeah."

Luckily, Chris was rendered speechless. So was Nick.

"So that was our yesterday," Sophie said with a smirk. "How was your day?"

We went on to tell them about the newspaper articles Sophie had found, and the revelation that Ernest and Hazel had a daughter. Neither of the brothers had ever seen Clara in or around the house. As they'd told us before, they'd never seen *anyone* in or around the house. Just Shade.

"I feel really bad," Chris said as we walked back home, dragging our sleds behind us along the slushy sidewalks.

"Why?" Nick asked.

"I can't stop wondering what happened to Clara. What if she was just a little kid when her parents both died? What if she was younger than us?"

"Imagine if Mom and Dad died," Sophie said to me, a note of sadness in her voice. "What would happen to us?"

I shrugged. I'd never thought about that before. Without realizing it, I guess I'd always thought Mom and Dad were invincible. "I dunno. We'd go live with Grandpa or Aunt Susan and Uncle Hank, I guess."

"If we get to pick," Sophie said, "I'd want to move in with Aunt Susan and Uncle Hank."

"Why?"

"They have a bigger TV."

"True, but Grandpa lives in Florida, two hours from Disney World."

"Ooh, you're right. Grandpa wins."

"They don't seem too upset that their parents just died," Nick said to Chris with a smile and a nudge.

But Chris didn't look like he was in a joking mood. "I just feel bad for Clara and wonder where she went." His eyes grew moist, and he wiped his nose with the back of his glove. "It reminds me of Andrea," he added so softly I barely heard him.

"Who's Andrea?" I asked quietly. I had a feeling it was a very personal question, but Chris had brought it up.

Nick answered for his brother. "She was—"

"Is," Chris interrupted.

"*Is* our baby sister. She died."

Sophie gasped.

"I'm so sorry," I said.

"It's okay," Nick said. "It happened three years ago. She died at birth."

"I'm sorry, too," Sophie said. "That's terrible."

"It *was* terrible," Chris said. "It seemed like forever before Mom and Dad started to return to normal, and even now they argue a lot more than they used to."

I glanced at Nick. His eyes were squinted and his jaw was clenched.

Chris continued, "I always had the feeling that Andrea was alone somewhere. I was sure her soul or spirit or whatever you want to call it still existed, and she was alone and scared."

I thought Chris was on the verge of a full-blown mental breakdown, but then he wiped his nose again, shivered, and sighed, and the look of pain slowly slipped off his face.

Nick slapped his brother on the shoulder. "C'mon, let's warm up and play some video games. You guys wanna come?"

I was in no rush to go back home—not with ghosts in my room—but after Chris's sad story I thought it would be awkward going over there. But how could I say no without being obvious?

It didn't matter. Sophie spoke up in my silence. "Sure," she said.

Chris seemed better as soon as we walked in their house and powered up the game console. I grabbed a controller and tried to put the past few days out of my mind.

~⦿~

In hindsight, spending a few hours playing a game called *Kill Screen*, about a ghost hunter who investigates a seemingly never-ending string of haunted houses while battling all manner of ghosts, specters, poltergeists, and demons, wasn't the best way to keep Chris's mind off the loss of his sister, nor was it the best way to get over my fear of sleeping in my room with Danny's spirit in my closet.

Needless to say, I took Sophie up on her offer to sleep on her floor for a second night in a row.

"When we start school next week," I said as I slipped beneath the duvet, "please don't tell anyone about this."

"Your secret is safe with me."

"Thanks. And thanks."

"Two thanks?"

"For keeping the secret and for letting me sleep in here again."

"You're welcome. You can sleep in here as long as you like."

"But the longer I do, the sooner Mom and Dad will find out. And what do we say then? We've got to do something about Danny."

"He didn't seem all that bad," Sophie said.

"No, he didn't. But Jack creeps me out. Why didn't he come out? And why did Danny refuse to let me look in on him?"

Sophie nodded. "Yeah, Jack is super creepy." She grabbed the Batman comic from her bedside table and leafed through its pages. "What about this?" she said after a moment.

"What?" I sat up and peered over the edge of her bed at the comic resting on her lap.

She held up a page for me to see. "Nth metal. Batman has a whole bunch of weapons made out of it. It seems to be able to hurt Gentleman

Ghost and his horse. Maybe it would work on the Creightons and Shade, and even Danny."

I laid back down with a sigh. "Sure, that could work. Except for three things: we don't have any Nth metal, it's from outer space, and it's make-believe."

"Well, sorry for trying to help," Sophie said. She sounded hurt.

I sat back up. "I'm sorry. Thanks for trying."

She shrugged and turned on her phone, then typed something into it. "Oh, look at this," she said, scrolling on the screen. "I just Googled 'does metal repel ghosts?' Guess what the top website results are. 'Why Does Iron Repel Spirits? Paranormal Protection with Iron and Silver. Iron and Steel: Why Does It Damage Ghosts and Spirits?' I can go on, if you want."

I held up my hands and said, "I mean it: I'm sorry. I was rude, but I didn't mean to be."

But Sophie was no longer listening. She had turned her attention back to the comic.

I was about to apologize yet again when Sophie said, "Hm."

"What is it?" I asked.

"Nothing."

"No, seriously. What?"

Sophie sighed and said, "In the end, it's not Batman who defeats Gentleman Ghost. Not even Superman, Wonder Woman, or Green Lantern. It's Gentleman Ghost's own army of spirits that he was trying to control to do his bidding. They turn on him and pull him back down into something called the Netherworld."

Just then my phone dinged. A text message from Nick. It was only one word. One desperate, panicked word.

HELP!!!

CHAPTER 16

I IMMEDIATELY TEXTED BACK.

Where are you?

"What was that?" Sophie asked.

"Nick. He texted me asking for help."

"What's wrong?"

"I have no idea."

"Where is he?"

"I don't—"

My phone dinged again.

Your backyard

"Quick," I said to Sophie. "The backyard."

We ran quietly downstairs and grabbed our coats, threw on our boots, and went outside. The snow squeaked beneath our feet as we sprinted around the house to the backyard. I saw Nick immediately. He was standing up against the wall as if to stay out of the wind, or maybe he was trying to remain hidden.

He looked terrified, and his eyes were wide and wet. "What's wrong?" I asked, glancing up at our second-floor windows. Luckily, Mom and Dad's room was on the other side of the house, so I hoped they wouldn't hear us.

"He wasn't there," Nick said, shaking his head. "He just left. What was he thinking?"

"Who?" Sophie asked. "Chris?"

Nick nodded frantically. "We have to help him. We have to do something."

"Where did he go?" I asked. But I already knew.

Nick looked past Sophie and me and pointed over our shoulders.

The Creightons' house.

❧

Nick filled us in as we crept closer to Briar Patch Farm, searching for some sign of Chris in the field between our houses but finding none.

"He was still talking about Clara and Andrea as we went to bed. I tried to tell him that even if Clara was a baby when her parents died, she would've been looked after by someone else and would be an adult now, but he wouldn't listen to me. He was in his own world and kept repeating that he needed to find out the truth. I never thought he'd get up in the middle of the night and sneak out. I had this weird dream about him, so I went into his room, and it was empty."

"How do you know that he left the house?" I asked. "Could he be in the bathroom?"

"He'd stuffed pillows under his sheets to look like he was still in bed. You don't do that if you're going to pee."

"Look," Sophie said. She pointed at the street, brightly lit by streetlights. The asphalt was covered in a blanket of fresh snow that was undisturbed except for a few sets of tire tracks. At first that's all I noticed, but then I saw what had made Sophie stop. There was one set of footprints leading from Nick's house to ours, and another set from Nick's house to the Creightons'. I followed the path of the second set of footprints with my eyes—they went first up to the farmhouse's front door, then doubled back and went around to the backyard. They didn't come back to the front yard.

Nick groaned. "What have you done, Chris?"

I scanned the field and peered into the stable but saw no sign of Shade. That somehow made everything worse. I'd rather know what we were dealing with than not, and I had a feeling there was a lot we still didn't know about the house next door. It would have been easier to turn and leave.

It would have felt safer to hide in my house until morning and pretend nothing was wrong. But I couldn't do that. Chris and Nick were our friends—our only friends in the neighborhood.

We needed to help Chris. I needed to step up and be the type of person I admired so much in movies and books.

"I don't know what he's done, so there's only one thing to do," I told Nick. "Let's go find out."

CHAPTER 17

I LED SOPHIE AND NICK to the back of the Creightons' house, where we joined up with Chris's footprints. Each print was a long stride from the last. He'd run. The tracks led to a sliding basement window.

"There," I said, motioning the others to follow me.

The window was still open a crack. I slid it open the rest of the way. It would be a tight fit, but the three of us were small enough to squeeze through.

"C'mon," I said. "I'll go first."

"Wait, what's the plan?" Sophie asked.

"Plan?" Who had time to come up with a plan? "We go in, find Chris, and get out. That's it."

Sophie looked queasy but nodded in agreement.

Nick was still wide-eyed, but his nerves seemed to be calming down a little. "Thank you."

"Thank us once we've found your brother," I said.

The open window was like a large mouth waiting to swallow us up. A draft of air streamed out of the basement that somehow felt colder than the air outside. I couldn't see anything inside, only darkness.

Go in. Find Chris. Get out.

I hesitated. Could I actually do that? I had no idea what lay in wait in the old house.

Something touched my arm. I jumped. It was Sophie. She'd placed a hand on my shoulder and offered me a thin smile.

"You've got this," she said. "We're with you. WWBD?"

I nodded. My fears didn't vanish like in the movies. They were still very much within me, but they'd been pushed down and covered up. Hopefully they'd stay that way long enough to do what I had to do.

"WWBD," I said.

"WWBD?" Nick asked, clearly confused.

"Never mind," I said. And then, without wasting any more time, I slid through the window and into the darkness.

∽◌◠

I met my first surprise when my feet touched down. The ground was soft. Not concrete, like I had expected. Dirt. I took a step to the side and helped Sophie down, then offered a hand to Nick. He waved me off and jumped in on his own.

A soft beam of blue moonlight illuminated their faces but I couldn't see much else. My eyes needed time to adjust to the dark, but time was something I didn't have. Chris could be in danger. No, Chris was in danger. This was not a safe place, and he was alone. I pictured Danny and Jack in their beds, their bodies crushed, mangled, and bloodied. How much time did Chris have before the same thing happened to him?

We had to find him, and we had to find him fast. "If only we could follow his tracks," I said, "like we did in the snow."

"If only we could see," Nick added. "It's so dark in here."

"Do you guys have your phones on you?" Sophie said. "Mine's still in my room."

Nick and I both reached into our pockets and pulled out our phones. I turned on my light a moment before Nick.

Sophie smiled and raised her eyebrows. "Go on, say it," I said.

"Someone's gotta be the brains of the group."

I nodded. Nick and I scanned the basement. It revealed its secrets slowly.

The dirt floor was uneven. The walls were made of old crumbling stone. Pipes and rough wooden beams crisscrossed above our heads. A rickety staircase led up to the only door.

An old wood stove sat in one corner with a wide black pipe that ran through the ceiling. It wasn't producing any heat. My fingers throbbed from the cold. White clouds of fog streamed out of our mouths and noses with every breath.

Horseshoes hung from pegs on the wall and an assortment of gear—a couple of saddles, a pile of stirrups, leading ropes—was heaped on the ground.

I turned around and flinched. It took all my strength to not yell and drop my phone. A pair of black, dead eyes stared back at me from a face covered in cobwebs.

It was an old, homemade Santa Claus statue made out of papier mâché. His skin was wrinkled and cracked, and he appeared to have been chewed by mice over the years.

"That's the scariest Christmas decoration I've ever seen," I said.

"Scarier than anything I've ever seen on *Screamers*," Nick said.

Part of me wanted to turn my back on Santa and put him out of my mind, while another part wanted to keep both my light and my eyes on him to make sure he didn't blink or move the moment I looked away. After a brief internal struggle, I reluctantly moved on.

A bunch of old furniture was stored in a corner. Covered in dust were three wicker chairs, a small wooden table, and a floor lamp with no shade. Its light bulb was shattered. Jagged edges of glass jutted up from the lamp's socket.

"What a dump," Sophie said.

I agreed with Sophie; the place was a dump. The weird thing was that the lamp was plugged in. It was connected to an extension cord that ran up the wall and was plugged into an electrical outlet that was screwed into one of the ceiling's wooden beams.

"Hey, look at the lamp. The bulb is broken, but the cord's plugged in," I said, pointing at the outlet. "I think the table and chairs were set up to be used, and not just tossed down here for storage."

"Why would anyone want to sit down here in the dirt?" Sophie said.

Something big skittered across the floor between us and the furniture.

This time I yelled out in fear. So did Sophie and Nick.

It was an opossum the size of a large cat. Its fur was grey and wiry, and its snout was long and white. Its eyes, like Santa's, were as black as ink. It opened its mouth, exposed sharp, pointy teeth, and hissed at us. Then it scurried across the basement and knocked the Santa statue over as it fled.

I didn't have time to catch my breath or calm my nerves. Santa had been hiding something. In the corner behind the overturned statue, hammered into the dirt floor, were two wooden crosses.

"WHAT ARE THOSE?"

Sophie swallowed. "Crosses," she said quietly.

"Please tell me they're fake," Nick said. "You know, Halloween decorations."

"If they were decorations, they wouldn't be buried in the ground." I approached the crosses hesitantly. "There's a name carved into each one."

ERNEST CREIGHTON. HAZEL CREIGHTON.

Sophie shook her head in disbelief. "They're

buried in the basement? Not only is that gross, but the obituary said they were buried in a local cemetery."

An old, crinkled photograph was nailed into each cross. Ernest and Hazel's faces stared sternly back at me, their black-and-white eyes appearing to penetrate deep into my soul. It felt invasive and discomforting.

"They looked about the same age as their ghosts," Sophie said.

I held my light up to the pictures and looked a little closer at the Creightons. There was a bit of damage on Hazel's photo, right on her left cheek. Their eyes seemed to follow me as I moved the photos side to side. But despite that effect, and the feeling that they were looking into my soul, their eyes looked... "Their eyes look dead," I said. I dragged my nail over Hazel's left cheek, but I didn't feel any damage. I looked closer than I had before and felt my stomach drop. "These photos were taken after they died."

Sophie looked over my shoulder and groaned in disgust. "I think you're right."

"How can you be sure?" Nick asked.

I pointed at Hazel's cheek. "Her flesh was already decomposing when it was taken. You can see her teeth through this hole in her flesh."

It dawned on me that Hazel's hair was spread out around her head, resting on what appeared to be the same ground where she'd been buried. I looked down at my feet. "Is this the same floor as in the photos?" I asked.

Sophie and Nick looked at the photos, then the ground and then backed away from the crosses, watching very closely for any subtle movement in the dirt.

"She looks a little different than she did the other day," I said.

"Yeah," Sophie said, pointing at the photo. "That's a corpse. We talked to her ghost. You saw how Danny was able to change how he looked."

Being reminded of Danny, here in the

Creightons' basement while standing next to a couple of graves and looking at two pictures of dead people, raised my panic level to new heights.

Thump, thump, thump.

My heartbeat was so loud in my ears I wouldn't have been surprised if Sophie and Nick had been able to hear it.

Thump, thump, thump.

They had both fallen silent and their mouths gaped. They looked at each other, then at me.

I began to wonder if they actually *could* hear my heartbeat.

I was about to make a joke when Nick spoke. "You hear that?"

Sophie looked up at the ceiling. "Footsteps."

Thump, thump, thump.

❧

Nick and I both turned off our phones, and the three of us waited in the dark for what felt like an eternity. We didn't speak for fear of being discovered. But if anyone was in the basement with us, our heavy breathing would've given us away.

I was just about to ask the others what we should do when I heard a muffled conversation above our heads. I couldn't make out the words, but I heard two different voices—an old woman and a young, frightened boy.

"That's Chris," Nick said.

"And Hazel," Sophie added.

A light turned on upstairs and shone through the cracks around the basement door.

I raised a finger to my lips to show Sophie and Nick to be quiet, then gestured them to follow me. We crept up the stairs slowly, trying not to put too much weight on each step. One or two creaked loudly. I hoped the closed door was enough to block the noise.

As soon as I reached the top step, a pair of feet on the other side passed by and briefly cast shadows under the door. I froze until I heard Hazel speak again. I pressed my ear against the door. Sophie and Nick did the same on my right and left.

"You might as well talk," Hazel said, "since you can't leave."

"Please let me go," Chris said.

"I'll make you a deal: you tell me why you broke into my house, and I'll let you go."

Silence. I imagined Chris was deciding whether or not Hazel was telling the truth. "Do you promise?"

"Cross my heart and hope to die."

"Don't believe her, Chris," Nick whispered through his teeth.

Lie or not, Chris bought it. "Okay. My friends found out about you and Ernest. I came to find out what happened to your daughter."

"My daughter?" Hazel said with a chuckle. "Thank you. I was in need of a laugh. I don't get out much—well, ever." There was another pause and I imagined Hazel regarding Chris coolly.

"You said your friends found out about me and Ernest. What did you mean by that?"

"That he died after a couple of boys accidentally killed Shade. And that you and Ernest—the horse, too—are ghosts."

"You're a little right," she said slowly, "and a little wrong."

"Where is she?" Chris asked. "Where's Clara? Have you hurt her? Have you kept her locked somewhere in this house all these years since you died?"

"Clara is... Clara is fine," Hazel said. "Can I ask what you'd do if you found her, still alive and all grown up?" Pause.

"Don't do it, Chris," I said quietly. "Don't tell her the truth."

"I..." Chris said. "I would get her out of here. I'd call the police and tell them what is going on in this house."

"Thank you for being honest with me," Hazel said with a sigh. "Honesty is so rare these days, especially among children. Take, for example, those two boys who you said 'accidentally' killed Shade. They said they just wanted to go for a quick ride. They said they didn't mean to hurt Shade. They lied. Boys can't be trusted. They *meant* to hurt my horse."

"When did they tell you that? They were killed in their sleep by Shade's ghost."

"How do you know that? And please remember how I feel about honesty."

"Danny—the older brother—his ghost is still next door. He told my friends everything."

"Danny's ghost has been there all these years? He doesn't deserve to remain here. He should have been sent straight to the Netherrealm," Hazel said in disgust. "I believe you, so I'm going to pay you back by letting you in on a secret. Yes, Shade trampled them in their beds. But I was there, hiding in the hallway, when they pleaded for their lives and lied about what they'd done— yes, they tried reasoning with a horse, and a dead horse, no less. Like your attempt to rescue my *daughter*, that gave me a good laugh."

"You were there? And you let Shade kill them?"

"My dear boy," Hazel said. "I didn't let Shade kill them. I led him to do it. He always was such a good, obedient horse. Even in death. And now I believe it's time to prove that to you."

The sound of a chair scraping across the ground was followed by the crash of a second chair falling over.

Hazel said, "Let's take a short walk out back to the stable, shall we?"

CHAPTER 19

NICK GRABBED THE HANDLE, BUT I stopped him from opening the door.

"Wait," I said. "If we barge out there now, she'll have the upper hand."

"So you just want to stay here and do nothing?" Nick said, understandably angry.

"No," I said. "If we hurry, we can go back out the window, beat them to the stable, and ambush Hazel as soon as she enters." Even if we reached the stable first, I still had no idea how to stop a ghost. And I couldn't help but wonder and worry about where Ernest was. I hoped Nick and Sophie weren't as scared as I was.

Nick nodded, as did Sophie.

I pulled my phone out of my pocket as I walked back down the stairs. Not to light my way, but to make a call. "Things have gotten out of hand. We should've called the police sooner." I dialed 9-1-1 and stepped off the bottom step onto the dirt floor.

I held the phone to my ear and heard it ring once.

That was as far as the call got. My phone crackled and hissed and went dead.

At the same time, I felt an intense pain in my wrist. The sensation was cold, so cold it burned, and the icy feeling spread through my forearm, over my elbow and up to my shoulder. Sophie and Nick both screamed as loud as if someone had plunged a long knife deep into their chests. Maybe someone had—I couldn't move or turn my head to look. My entire body was rigid, like I'd suddenly turned into a statue.

Suddenly Ernest stepped into my line of sight, and I saw that he was holding my wrist. I yelled and tried to pull myself free, but his grip didn't falter. He held me in place as tightly as if my body had been set in concrete.

"You feel that?" Ernest rasped. "You can't move, can you?"

I tried to shake my head but couldn't, and managed to say, "No," through my tightly drawn lips. The icy burn had spread throughout my entire body. The pain was quickly becoming unbearable. My skin was cold—so cold—but it also felt like it was being electrified. Consciousness was slipping away.

"What you're experiencing is a 'death touch,' and I'm sure it's quite unpleasant. But don't worry, the pain won't last long, since you'll be dead soon. I did warn you that I'd kill you if you ever returned here."

I tried to beg and plead for my life, but I couldn't speak, not even a single word.

"Your phones will no longer work," Ernest said. "I can fry any electrical device in my vicinity, if I want—one of the advantages of being dead."

The basement was growing colder, blacker. *Death touch*, I thought deliriously. *Where have I...?* "Batman," I mumbled, unsure whether I'd actually spoken aloud or was still only thinking to myself. "Gentleman Ghost. Death touch. Nth metal. Horse. Horseshoe." I faded for a moment then snapped back awake. "Iron."

Ernest frowned and smiled at the same time. "Sounds like you're losing your mind. You've actually stayed conscious longer than I'd expected."

Sophie ran past us. Ernest watched her go without trying to stop her. He was probably too surprised to move, or maybe he simply didn't think she could do anything to harm him.

But I knew then that I had spoken out loud, and she had caught my meaning.

She grabbed a horseshoe off the wall and spun to face us. "Catch," she shouted as she threw the horseshoe like a Frisbee at Ernest. In his surprise he released my wrist, and I regained control of my body almost immediately. The horseshoe passed through his shoulder, and he howled in pain. Sophie tossed me a horseshoe and another to Nick, then picked up a final one for herself.

Ernest looked at each of us, armed as we were, and retreated back to his grave, where he vanished through the dirt.

"Matt, you're a genius!" Sophie said.

"What just happened?" Nick said in disbelief, staring at his horseshoe as if it was the first one he'd ever seen in his life.

"Old horseshoes like these are made of iron," Sophie said. "Some people think iron repels ghosts. Well, I guess now we know it does."

Feeling was slowly working its way back

through my body as the pain from Ernest's grasp slowly faded away.

"What was that stuff you said about Batman and a gentleman and some sort of metal?" Nick asked me.

I briefly filled him in, then added, "Like Ernest, Gentleman Ghost calls his power a 'death touch.' It made me think that if that was the same, maybe the same things that hurt one ghost would also hurt the other. And since we didn't have any Nth metal in the basement I hoped that the horseshoes would work the same way."

"But how did you know they'd be made from iron?" Sophie asked.

"I didn't. I had no idea what metal horseshoes are made of." I shrugged. "But we had nothing to lose. It's strange that a horseshoe stopped a ghost who loves horses so much. Think it will work on Shade?"

"It's worth a shot," Sophie said. "We still have nothing to lose."

"Chris!" Nick suddenly shouted. "We've lost too much time. There's no way we can beat Hazel to the stable and surprise her now."

"You're right. We can't beat her there." I held my horseshoe up for a moment and then tucked it into the front of my pants, pulling my jacket down over it to conceal it from view. "But we can still surprise her."

Nick and Sophie followed my lead and hid their horseshoes. I picked up the horseshoe Sophie had thrown at Ernest and hung it over his cross.

"Hopefully that will keep him buried in his grave," I said.

Nick picked up the creepy Santa statue and placed it under the open window. I climbed on the statue's head and pulled myself through the opening, then turned back and pulled Sophie up. Nick came next. I grabbed his hand and helped him as he climbed up the wall. Something caught my eye as I pulled him outside, but I shook it off.

"What?" he asked as we both got to our feet beside Sophie.

"Nothing," I said. "C'mon." But it hadn't been nothing.

Over Nick's shoulder, as I'd pulled him out, I'd caught a flicker of movement down in the basement. Ernest's cross had trembled, and the horseshoe I'd placed there had nearly slipped off.

I cast one last wary look through the basement window and followed Nick and Sophie toward the stable.

CHAPTER 20

"I FEEL LIKE I'M GOING to be sick to my stomach," Nick said as we crept across the field. He slipped on a patch of ice and fell to his knee. His horseshoe fell beside him.

I grabbed him under one arm and helped him up, feeling sorry for him as I did. He'd already lost one younger sibling, and now the other was in danger.

"Thank you," Nick said as he rose to his feet.

"What are friends for?"

Sophie dug his horseshoe out of the snow and wiped it off, then handed it back to him.

"Yeah," Nick said as we reached the stable. "It's good to have friends."

Hopefully we weren't too late.

From within the stable, Shade's neigh cut through the night.

Nick ran into the stable first, with Sophie and me close at his heels. We kept our iron horseshoes hidden for the moment. There was no sign of Hazel or Shade.

A bright circle of light from an overhead bulb illuminated the center of the stable. And sitting on the ground at the edge of the circle was Chris, tied to a wooden pillar. His head perked up when we entered.

"Nick!" he said excitedly, then he noticed my sister and me. "You came for me!"

"Of course we came for you, bro," Nick said.

We ran to Chris's side and kneeled around him. Nick began untying the rope that held Chris in place.

"Make that quick," Chris said. "She'll be back any—"

"Minute?" a female voice said. Hazel walked around a corner from the back aisle where the horse stalls were located. She led Shade by a rope. "Or were you going to say 'second'? That would be more accurate, because voilà! Here I am."

I nearly grabbed my horseshoe but had to remind myself to leave it hidden until Hazel was close enough to strike. Sophie and Nick left theirs hidden for the time being, too.

"I know you two," Hazel said, her eyes drifting over Sophie and me. Her gaze settled on Nick. "But who are you?"

"I'm Chris's brother," Nick said. "And I'm getting him out of here."

"No, you're not," Hazel said. "Hands off the rope."

"No."

"With one word from me, Shade will charge and crush the four of you before you even know what happened. Hands. Off." Hazel made a soft clicking sound with her tongue and gently tugged on the rope, as if to make a point. Shade snorted loudly and stamped one of his front hooves on the ground. I could feel the floor shake from where I sat and had no doubt Shade could kill us in a heartbeat if Hazel commanded him.

Nick slowly released the rope. Chris was still tied to the pillar.

"Good boy," Hazel said.

"If you could kill us right now, why wait?" Sophie asked.

"Kill four children at once?" Hazel said with mock surprise. "That seems a little dark and morbid, even by my standards. I think I'll let one or two of you live, but I haven't yet decided whom to spare."

Why would she be so quick to kill any of us? Just because Danny and Jack had killed Shade? Because Sophie had tried to feed the horse? Because Chris had snuck over here to find out what happened to Clara? Something didn't add up. There was more to Hazel's story, I just didn't know what.

She led Shade closer. His eyes glowed faintly blue.

"Then again," Hazel continued, "you all know too much, so the decision might be out of my hands."

They walked close enough to easily hit them with an accurate throw, so I yelled, "Now!" and revealed my horseshoe. Sophie and Nick did the same.

Shade reared up on his hind legs and whinnied frantically. He kicked the air with his front legs and then backed away snorting.

"Whoa, whoa, whoa," Hazel said, trying to calm her horse. "It's okay, boy. I won't let them hurt you."

"Oh yeah?" Nick said, emboldened by the

horse's evident fear. "Just try to stop us." He threw the horseshoe at Shade.

Shade pulled free from Hazel in a blind panic, but Hazel stepped in front of her horse and caught the horseshoe.

"What?" I said. "How did you—"

"Catch this?" Hazel asked, looking at the horseshoe in her hand and then back at us. "Iron only works on ghosts."

"But you're—"

"Not a ghost."

Not a ghost. The words clanged around inside my skull, impossible to comprehend but refusing to be ignored. "That doesn't make sense. Your husband died twenty years ago and he looked just as old then as you do now. Shouldn't you look a whole lot...?"

Hazel looked slightly wounded but maintained her composure. She cupped her cheek and slowly dragged her fingertips to her chin. She said nothing.

Sophie picked up where I had left off. "Yeah, you should look much, much older. And I read a newspaper article that said you died before your husband. Was that a lie?"

Hazel nodded and sighed. "All right, you got me. That article was correct. Hazel died twenty years ago."

"What do you mean?" Nick said. He looked as confused as I felt.

"I am not Hazel," she said, and it felt like the ground had been pulled out from beneath my feet. "I'm her daughter."

CHAPTER 21

"CLARA," CHRIS SAID FROM THE floor. "You're Clara."

Clara looked at Sophie and me and said, "When you showed up at my door with your cookies and assumed I was my mother, I was taken by surprise. Angry, too. Do I really look that old? The years since my father's death have simply slipped away. I rarely go out, never allow anyone in, and don't even like looking in the mirror. But I realized it wasn't surprising you'd mistake me for my mother. I'm the same age she was when she died."

"Why didn't you say anything?" I asked. "Why didn't you correct us?"

"What would be the point? I had no plans to see either of you ever again. Not after I killed you, that is."

"What?" Sophie said. She gripped her horseshoe a little tighter.

Clara laughed once—a sharp, piercing sound that echoed off the stable's wooden walls. "I couldn't just let you live. You had tried to take Shade once, and I knew it was only a matter of time before you tried again, just like those evil brothers did before. I already lost him before, and I'll die before I lose him again."

"Sophie didn't try to take your horse, and we definitely don't want anything to do with Shade now." I spoke slowly, hoping my words would sink in. But I doubted anything I could say would get through to her at this point.

I was right.

"Drop your horseshoes," she said.

"We don't want—"

Clara cut me off. "Drop. Your. Horseshoes."

I nodded at Sophie. She nodded back. We dropped our horseshoes. They clanged loudly on the floor.

"Now kick them to me."

We did as we were told, sliding the horseshoes with the toes of our shoes. Mine slid straight across to Clara while Sophie's stopped a little less than halfway.

"If none of you struggle, this will be over soon. But it won't be painless, I'm afraid. Far from it." She turned and faced Shade, then raised her hand in the air. She was going to signal him to run each of us down, and there'd be nothing we could do to stop him.

"Wait!" I shouted.

Clara looked at me. She didn't seem overly annoyed by the interruption. If anything, she looked eager, like this was all just a game to her, a game she couldn't lose.

I could only think of one thing that might save Sophie and me—one desperate thing.

"Danny and Jack," I said, "the brothers who killed Shade. It's not fair that their souls have been able to live on after what they did, don't you think?" I didn't bother pausing to allow her to answer. "What if I was able to trick their ghosts to come over here so you could be rid of them forever? Would you let me and my sister go?"

I looked straight at Clara, avoiding eye contact with Nick and Chris. But I couldn't avoid hearing my sister.

"Matt! What are you doing?" Her voice was quiet, baffled, and wounded.

I didn't acknowledge her.

Clara stared at me skeptically, as if she was trying to get a read on me. After a tense moment, she said, "I can't release all four of you. There has to be payback for breaking into my house and threatening Shade."

I closed my eyes and swallowed. "I know. Just Sophie and me."

Following one final pause, Clara said, "Deal. Go get Danny and Jack and bring them back here, and I'll let you and your sister go."

"I can't believe this," Nick said, full of rage. "You've got to be joking."

Chris sounded like he was in shock. "Unreal."

"No way, Matt," Sophie said. "You can't do this. We can't just—"

"Yes, we can," I said, interrupting her. "C'mon, let's go."

"No, no, no," Clara said. "Not so fast. I can't let you both leave." She pointed at me. "You go get Danny and Jack." Then she pointed at Sophie. "She'll stay here with me. I'll give you fifteen minutes. If you return with the twins, I'll let you and your sister go. And if not—or if you tell anyone; your parents, the police—she'll be the first to die." My jaw tensed, and I ground my teeth together.

"Fine." I didn't like it, but I didn't have a choice.

"Tick, tock," Clara said.

I caught a glimpse of Sophie. She didn't look mad or scared or even sickened. She looked disappointed. I didn't blame her. I'd let her down, and in a big way.

It hurt to see Sophie look at me like that.

But it had to be done. I wasn't going to stand by and do nothing. I wasn't going to let anything bad happen to my sister, no matter the cost.

I turned and ran out of the stable. I didn't look back.

CHAPTER 22

"DANNY?" I CALLED IN THE darkness of my room. I stared at my closet door, closed tight. "Jack?"

Nothing happened. The door didn't open, and neither ghost made a sound. What if they were no longer in there? What if they'd moved on or something?

That wasn't an option. They had to be in my closet. They *had* to be. And if they weren't going to come out, I was going to go in.

My hand shook as I reached out to turn the

handle. I took a deep breath and steadied my shakes. *Get a grip*, I told myself. *Sophie's life is at stake.*

Before any more doubt or fear could stop me, I threw open the door and stepped into the closet.

Only, it wasn't my closet.

Somehow, I'd opened the closet door in my bedroom and stepped into an entirely different closet in an entirely different room in an entirely different house. My closet was wide and shallow; this one was narrow and deep. It was filled with clothes for a boy my age—hanging on the left were sweaters and shirts and on the right was a matching collection.

Identical clothes for identical twins.

I was in Danny and Jack's closet. But I had no time to be scared. I'd come to collect them, after all. I stepped into the room—the twins' room, not mine—and scanned my surroundings. The carpet was bloodred and the walls covered in dark brown wood paneling, which in turn were covered in old movie posters from the 1980s and 1990s: *The Empire Strikes Back*, *Indiana Jones and the Last Crusade*, *Back to the Future*, *Jurassic Park*. Danny and Jack had the same taste in movies as me and my dad. It didn't make what I had to do any easier.

"Danny? Jack?" I called again. Once again I was answered with silence.

But the silence didn't last.

Clip, clop. Clip, clop. Clip, clop.

Horse hooves. In the hallway.

Clip, clop. Clip, clop. Clip, clop.

Getting closer. Right outside the door.

Clip, clop. Clip, clop. Clip, clop.

My breath caught in my throat and I looked wildly around the room. In my panic I jumped into one of the beds and threw the covers over my head. It was probably the worst place I could have chosen to hide, but too late.

The door creaked open. Shade snorted.

He took his time crossing the room—*Clip, clop.*

Clip, clop. Clip, clop—as if he was drawing the moment out and savoring the flavor of my fear.

He's not real, he's not real, he's not real, I told myself. None of this is real. It's all in your mind, like when you saw Sophie trampled in her bed. When you look again you won't be in Danny and Jack's room.

I looked again, but oh, how I was wrong.

I was still in Danny and Jack's room, and Shade was very much in the room with me. He towered above the bed, impossibly large and staring down on me with anger. He raised up onto his two back legs, whinnied, bucked his front legs in the air two or three times, then came kicking down on top of me.

꘎꘎꘎

I opened my eyes and sat bolt upright in bed and readied to scream—but stopped. I was back in my own bed, back in my own room. Scared, stressed, and covered in sweat, but alive. Shade was gone. The *vision* of Shade was gone, I corrected myself.

How much time had passed? Five minutes? More? Either way, I couldn't have much time left before Clara...

The closet door opened.

Slowly, Danny stepped out. His body wasn't trampled and bloodied like the first time I'd seen him exit my closet, but the sight of a ghost entering my room still sent shivers down my spine.

"Danny," I said. "Where's your brother? I need to speak to you both."

"I told you, he's—"

"Easily startled," I finished. There wasn't time to waste. I had to cut to the chase. "Shade's ghost wasn't commanded by Mr. Creighton to kill you and your brother. His daughter, Clara, was responsible. She still lives in Briar Patch Farm, with the ghosts of her horse and father. They... they have my sister, and they're going to kill her. But listen, Danny..."

His expression had remained calm and unemotional as I spoke, and I knew I had to sell the next part if I'd be able to convince Danny and Jack to help me.

"I think I know how to send Shade back to the Netherrealm and take down Clara."

Danny finally reacted the way I had hoped—he smiled, and I knew he'd help me.

I told him then, as quickly as possible, what had happened and what we needed to do. I left out the parts where I had sold out the Russos in order to save Sophie and, of course, that I had promised to hand Danny and Jack over to Clara in exchange for my sister. Those two details would have done nothing to help convince the twin ghosts to follow me to the farm.

Luckily, it wasn't difficult convincing Danny to follow me. He seemed ready to fly through my bedroom wall and straight outside if I hadn't told him to wait for me. He didn't even pause to question whether or not I was telling the truth—he believed everything I told him and was eager to help.

"I'll do it for me," he said, "but more for Jack."

"For this to work, we need him, too. Can you call him out?"

"Can we do it without him? He's—"

"No, Danny," I stared hard at Danny and spoke sternly. "He *needs* to come."

Danny looked at the closet and sighed. "That's going to be a problem."

Somehow I knew without him saying it. "Jack's not here, is he?"

Danny shook his head. "As soon as we were killed, Jack passed on. Only I remained."

CHAPTER 23

IT DIDN'T MATTER. THE PLAN would work without Jack. I'd promised Clara both brothers, but that was before I'd known Jack had already moved on.

I had to hope.

But try as I might to ignore the sinking feeling in my gut, it was there all the same.

"We heard whispering," I told Danny. "Sophie and me. We both heard you whispering to someone in my closet, the first night we saw you."

"I...talk to Jack sometimes. Maybe often. It

helps me. I know he's not there, but I don't care. It makes me feel less lonely."

The past couple of nights I'd been too afraid to sleep in my own room thanks to Danny's creepy presence, but now I felt sorry for him. He wasn't someone to fear. He was someone I wished I could help.

Maybe I could.

I checked the time. We only had a few minutes left. "We have to go," I said.

After a quick dash into Sophie's room I grabbed her phone (mine was fried, permanently). Danny and I crept to the stairs. My parents' bedroom light was still off. It was a lucky thing they were such deep sleepers—they'd had lots of opportunities over the past few nights to wake up and catch Sophie and me sneaking around. I briefly considered waking them—I needed help— but Clara had made it very clear that she'd kill my sister if I told anyone. So telling them was out of the question.

I told Danny to follow me outside and raced into the Creightons' field.

We stopped beside the stable doors so I could catch my breath and steel my nerves. This was it, the moment of truth, and I knew I wouldn't come out on top if I went in nervous.

Would Batman feel sick to his stomach at this moment? Of course not, but I was no hero. I was just a kid scared out of his mind and trying to save his sister.

Danny tapped me on the shoulder. His touch spread a chill over my skin like frost forming on a window. He pointed to the field past the stable.

There was another cross like the pair in the basement with a different name carved on it: Shade.

"Jeez," I said. "Doesn't Clara send any of her bodies to the morgue or...wherever you send dead horses?"

Danny didn't seem to hear me. He was too absorbed in his own thoughts. "I still feel really bad about what happened with Shade. Things got out of hand."

"I know," I said, resisting the urge to place my hand on Danny's shoulder. I was still chilled from his touch. "But that was still no excuse for what Clara and Shade did to you and your brother. And if you do this—if you help me—you'll stop them from hurting anyone else."

Danny nodded. "I hope I get to see Jack again."

"Why do you think you stayed and he didn't?"

"I think it was because...because it was my idea in the first place to take Shade for a ride. It was all my fault. He wasn't just my brother. He was my best friend."

"You'll be reunited with him soon," I said. "Do you remember what we talked about in my room? What we need to do?"

He nodded again, this time with resolve.

And I knew he was committed. Maybe—just maybe—this would work. I took a step toward the door.

"Wait," Danny said. "Before you go in, I just want to say thank you."

"Thank *you*," I replied.

And then I stepped into the stable, hopefully for the last time.

The scene was pretty much as I had left it. Clara stood beside Shade on one side of the stable, and Chris was still tied to a pillar in the middle. Nick and Sophie were kneeling on either side of him. Everyone looked at me as soon as I walked into the light. The looks on my sister's face and those of the Russo brothers appeared angry enough to kill.

I stopped just inside the open doorway. "Where are the twins?" Clara asked.

I shook my head and raised my arms, pleadingly. "They're still in my room. I couldn't convince them to come. I think they knew I was up to something. They were suspicious that I was setting a trap."

Clara shook her head. "I'm sorry to hear that. We had a deal."

"Yes, but give me time and I'm sure I'll be able to convince them, somehow, to come over here."

"That's not how this works," Clara said. "The deal was you had fifteen minutes to return with Danny and Jack, and I'd let you and your sister go. And if you didn't, well, your sister would be the first to die. That was the deal. And now I'm afraid I have no choice but to honor my end of the bargain."

Without looking at me, Sophie stood slowly and faced Clara and Shade. The action spoke loud and clear: *I'm not afraid of you.*

Clara laughed at Sophie's show of defiance, but I thought I detected a note of concern in the sound. She looked over her shoulder at Shade.

Shade snorted and stamped his hoof, preparing to charge.

Sophie stood her ground.

Clara raised her hand. "Shade," she said, then lowered her hand like an executioner's axe. "Kill."

CHAPTER 24

"WAIT!" I SHOUTED, BREAKING THE tension.

Clara's eyes flicked to me, and she looked ready to charge me herself, but there was curiosity there, too. She raised her hand again, this time to stop Shade, and the horse obeyed her.

I breathed a sigh of relief. "If I had been able to convince Danny and Jack to come over here, would you actually have let my sister and me go?"

Clara regarded me for a moment as if weighing

out the pros and cons of being truthful. I had already guessed what her answer would be.

"You already know, don't you?" she asked.

I didn't answer, didn't even nod. The longer I could draw this out, the better. It gave Danny more time to get into position.

"No, I never intended to let you and your sister go. How could I? You know too much. You've seen too much. You'd tell your parents, and I'd have the police banging down my front door like that." Clara snapped her fingers.

I laughed. It was fake, but Clara didn't know that and she took the bait.

"What's so funny?"

"Nothing, really. It's just, if that had happened, I wouldn't be using my phone. It was fried in your basement when Ernest confronted us."

"You were in my basement?" Clara roared. "You saw my father?"

"Yeah, that's where we first discovered that iron horseshoes repel ghosts. And I gotta say, it's a little weird you buried your parents in your basement."

"I dug them up from the cemetery and brought them home to be with me, where they belong!"

I pictured Clara sitting in the damp darkness with her parents' decomposing corpses and her father's ghost, and knew that's why the furniture had been set up down there.

"Sadly, my mother's ghost didn't come back with my father's," Clara said. "But dear old Dad, like Shade, died with unfinished business. They were eager to return...for revenge."

"Ernest is dead," I said. "Well, dead again. We pinned him down with iron horseshoes until he evaporated before our eyes. And since I couldn't get Danny and Jack to come over here with me, I'm going to grab one of those horseshoes and do the same to your horse."

My lie about evaporating Ernest and my threat of killing Shade worked. Clara locked eyes with me, and I could feel her fury radiating off her like heat waves. She was enraged, desperate, and irrational.

And all of her hatred was focused straight at me.

"You," she said. She wrinkled her nose and pulled her lips back as if addressing me physically repulsed her. "Shade! Charge!"

Shade rocketed toward me—not Sophie—like a cannonball. White froth spewed from his mouth, and he neighed loudly. His hooves thundered so forcefully that I could feel the ground shake from across the stable. *Ba da rump, ba da rump, ba da rump!*

I stood my ground. When Shade was only a few feet away I shouted, *"Danny! Now!"*

Danny slipped through the roof and dropped through the air. He landed on Shade's back and grabbed the reins. He didn't pull back or try to slow Shade—instead, he spurred the horse forward at a faster clip.

I jumped to the side just in time before being run down.

Danny rode Shade through the open doorway. Everything was going according to plan. Everything was going perfectly.

It didn't last.

Through the open stable doors, I caught a glimpse of a man approaching from the farmhouse.

Ernest.

CHAPTER 25

HOW HAD ERNEST GOTTEN PAST the horseshoe? I had seen it wobble, but not fall. And then a quick image flashed before my eyes, as realistic as the two hallucinations I'd had before. After we'd left the basement, the opossum had skittered out of its hiding place and bumped into the cross, knocking the horseshoe to the ground. I didn't know how I knew, but I knew that was what had happened.

And my hatred for that opossum reached new heights.

But there was no time to think about it. Ernest had nearly reached the stable. If he got in, not only would he be able to attack us, but I didn't know how to get him all the way back to his grave. And even if I could achieve that, he'd probably just escape again.

"Sophie!" I yelled. "Throw me that horseshoe!" I pointed at the one she had kicked toward Clara, the one that had only made it halfway across the stable.

Without hesitating, she picked it up and threw it to me.

I caught it and ran outside, straight toward Ernest.

I think the boldness of my charging him caught him off guard. He frowned and slowed his pace. That was good.

"Danny!" I shouted as I ran. "I need your help!"

He was galloping away fast, but he heard me over Shade's thundering hooves and looked back over his shoulder. Seeing what was happening, he pulled Shade in an arc, circling Ernest and me.

I didn't slow down. At the last possible second—right before colliding with Ernest—I raised the horseshoe and slammed it into his chest. With my free hand I grabbed hold of his shirt and pulled him toward Shade's grave.

Shocked, Ernest yelled and stumbled, allowing me to drag him to my intended target. But at the same time he grabbed the back of my neck, and my body tensed with pain. I closed my eyes tight, grunted in agony, and forced my legs to keep moving, hoping that I was still heading in the right direction. My stomach churned, my head throbbed, and I felt like I'd pass out at any moment.

Thankfully, it was enough.

I felt bumpy earth beneath my feet and opened my eyes to see that I'd managed to pull Ernest to Shade's grave.

Ernest's grave had acted as a portal before. I

could only hope Shade's would act the same way—and on a one-way, permanent basis this time.

I dropped to the ground and pulled Ernest down with me. He landed on his side, our faces only a few centimeters apart. A small white dot flickered deep in each of his irises, but otherwise his eyes were cold. The sight chilled my blood.

Fortunately, it was the last I saw of him.

Danny rode Shade straight through the ground and disappeared into the grave, first crushing, then pulling Ernest into the earth with them.

A deathly silence stretched out across the field. The wind died, and it started to snow. I held my breath and stared at the grave, worrying I'd see either Shade or Ernest come kicking and crawling back up through the dirt, but that didn't happen.

Danny thought he'd be able to keep them in the Netherrealm and prevent them from coming back, but I placed the horseshoe on the ground, just in case.

Feet pounded across the snow behind me. "Matt! Watch out!" Sophie shouted.

I spun and jumped out of the way. Clara dropped to her knees before Shade's grave. Sophie, Nick, and Chris stood behind her.

All the anger and hatred had drained out of Clara's face, leaving behind pale skin, sunken eyes, and quivering lips. Her shoulders were hunched, and she bent forward at the waist as if her body was broken and hollow. She buried her face in her hands, and then she began to cry.

She didn't appear to be a threat anymore, so I joined my sister and the Russo brothers.

"I am so, so sorry," I told them.

"It's all right," Chris said, raising his hand to prevent me from saying anything else.

"I'm not going to lie," Nick said. "I was super angry when I thought you were selling us out."

"I've never been so angry in my life," Sophie said.

Nick continued. "But now we know it was all part of your plan."

Sophie looked at Clara, then at the grave. "Are they gone for good? Ernest and Shade? And Danny, too?"

"I hope so," I said.

"How did you know Danny would be able to ride Shade into the ground?"

"I didn't. But I couldn't think of anything else, so I figured it was worth a shot. Remember that Batman comic book? I figured if iron worked in the real world the way Nth metal worked in the comic, maybe a ghost with a grudge would be able to force Shade—and Ernest—back to the place they belong. In the comic it was called the Netherworld. It stuck in my mind thanks to Sophie—she pointed it out earlier tonight."

Sophie beamed.

I lowered my voice a notch or two. "Clara called it the Netherrealm. I guessed that they were similar places, and that Ernest and Shade could be forced there by another ghost. Luckily, Danny really wanted to see his brother—Jack's ghost moved on as soon as he died—and he wanted to make sure Ernest and Shade couldn't hurt any more kids."

Clara continued to sob with her back to us.

"So basically," Sophie said, "your love of superheroes saved us."

"WWBD," Chris said.

"What would Batman do?" Nick said with a nod and a smile. "You're such a geek."

I shrugged and returned the smile.

"It saved our lives," Sophie said. "Wait until Dad hears that you used your geekiness for good. He's going to be so proud. Dad's a huge geek, too," she added for Nick and Chris's benefit.

I hadn't taken my eyes off Clara as we spoke. Her cheeks were wet, and her eyes were red. She didn't look at us or say a word. It was as if she was in her own world.

"When I went next door, I grabbed this," I said, as I took Sophie's phone out of my pocket.

"Didn't it get fried when you entered the stable?" Sophie asked.

I turned it on. I didn't know her passcode, but there were three bars on the top of the screen, so it had a signal. "I guess ghosts only do that if they mean to, not just by getting too close to a phone." I held the phone out for Sophie. "Anyway, can you call the police?"

Sophie didn't have time to take the phone.

Clara quickly got to her feet and lunged at me. Her fingers wrapped around my throat and squeezed.

CHAPTER 26

THE WORLD HAD SHIFTED ONCE more. It was no longer night. It was no longer winter. But I was still standing in the field at Briar Patch Farm.

The farmhouse and stable were the same but in better condition, and the field and gardens were in much better shape. There was only one other house nearby, but it looked nothing like ours. The two homes were surrounded by grassy hills, trees, and bushes.

There was a car in the driveway and,

hammered into the ground beside the curb, a FOR SALE sign. I approached the front of the house just as the door opened and Ernest and Hazel stepped out into the sunlight. Hazel held a small sign that said SOLD.

A moment later, Clara followed. She looked about twenty years younger than I was used to, about forty years old.

I didn't bother hiding. They looked right through me.

"So, what do you think?" Ernest asked Clara.

"I love it," Clara said. "But don't ask me. This has always been her dream. What do you think, Mom?" Hazel smiled with her mouth *and* her eyes.

"It's perfect." She spread her arms and her grown daughter eagerly flung herself into the embrace as if she was four years old, not forty. "I've always wanted to live in the country. And after I read *Black Beauty* when I was eight years old, I've always wanted to have a horse."

"I'm pleased for you," Clara said. "I'm pleased for *us*. We're going to be so happy here." She let go of her mother and looked quickly back at the house. "I forgot my purse inside. I'll be right back." She stepped back into the house.

Hazel's smile faltered as she turned to Ernest and gave him a meaningful look, but he held up his hands and stopped her from saying whatever she had been thinking.

"She can live with us as long as she needs to," he said. "I stopped thinking she should live on her own years ago. If you're both happy, I'm happy. That's honestly all I want."

Hazel's smile returned. "Thank you, Ernest." They hugged and she added, "This is a dream come true. I think I'm going to need to pinch my arms every morning 'til the day I die to make sure it's real."

Ernest waited on the porch for Clara to return, and Hazel walked to the street.

Neither Hazel nor Ernest saw the pickup truck

that turned the corner at the end of the country road. It swerved wildly and nearly drove off the road, then righted itself and continued toward Briar Patch Farm.

Hazel placed the small SOLD sign on the larger FOR SALE one. She sighed, a satisfied sound.

Then she frowned. So did Ernest.

They looked down the street, toward the sound of the approaching truck.

"Hazel?" Ernest said, shielding his eyes from the sun. He took a step toward her.

"He's driving awfully fast," Hazel said quietly.

"Hazel?" Ernest repeated, a little louder than before.

Clara stepped outside. The truck accelerated.

"Hazel!" Ernest shouted.

She didn't move. The truck veered left. It jumped the curb.

It drove into her, and she flipped over the hood, then landed on the front lawn. The driver didn't slow down. He drove back onto the street and sped away, kicking up a cloud of dirt in the truck's wake.

"Hazel, no!"

"Mom!"

Ernest and Clara ran to Hazel's side and knelt in the grass beside her. Blood ran out of her mouth, but she was still breathing.

"This can't be happening," Clara said. Tears streamed down her flushed cheeks. "Tell me this isn't real."

Ernest seemed paralyzed.

"Promise me," Hazel said softly. She seemed to know she'd been hurt too badly to recover.

"Anything," Clara said.

"I want to know you'll be happy. Promise me you'll still move here. Promise me—" She coughed, and more blood trickled down her chin. "Promise me you'll get the horse."

Clara closed her eyes tight and nodded. "I promise."

"Do you remember the name I always wanted?"

Clara nodded again. Tears fell from her chin. "Shade. I'll never let anything happen to him, as long as I live."

And as I watched the scene, the sky and the grass and the farmhouse and Ernest and Hazel faded away, leaving Clara behind in a crumpled heap before she disappeared as well.

The world returned, cold and dark once more.

It took a moment for me to get my bearings. I was lying on the ground, my back on the snow. Sophie looked down at me.

"Matt!" she shouted. "You're all right!"

"I'm fine," I said, sitting up and rubbing my head. "What happened? How long have I been out for?"

"A few minutes," she said. "You fainted as soon as she touched you." Sophie pointed at Clara, held back by Nick and Chris. With her head slumped, and her eyes closed, she wasn't putting up a fight. All the same, I hoped the Russos wouldn't relax their grips for a second.

I didn't think I'd fainted, not exactly. The vision—that was the closest word for what I'd seen—was stronger, more real, than those I'd had before. I hoped I never had another.

"Good news: my phone still works," Sophie said. "I called 9-1-1 as soon as they pulled Clara off you and you didn't wake up. They'll be here soon."

"Best news I've heard all week," I said, rubbing my pounding head. "Mind if I borrow your phone? I think it's time we tell Mom and Dad what's happened."

"Everything?"

"Everything."

"Even that we've decided to move to Florida when they die?"

"Maybe not *everything*."

CHAPTER 27

"ARE YOU TWO EXCITED FOR your first day at your new school tomorrow?" Mom asked from across the breakfast table.

"Does a one-legged duck swim in circles?" Sophie asked.

We'd spent far more time inside our house than outside during the remainder of March break. Mom had been too frightened to let us out of her sight, and the truth was I didn't mind. Neither did Sophie. The first few days in our new home had exhausted us, especially the final confrontation with Clara, Ernest, and Shade. But now we were both itching to get out and do something, anything. School included. I'd take a full day of math classes over another day spent cooped up inside, plus I was looking forward to seeing Nick and Chris again. Their parents had also kept them in their house for the rest of the week. We'd been texting each other on our new phones.

"Hot stuff coming through!" Dad shouted. He crossed the kitchen carrying a frying pan in one hand and a spatula in the other. "And no, I'm not just talking about your breakfast." He looked at us for a moment, and when no one replied he added, "I'm referring to me. I'm the hot stuff."

"Yeah, we get it," Mom said with a smile.

But Dad wasn't the type to let jokes that had fallen flat get him down. He flipped a couple of pancakes out of the pan and onto our plates.

I stared down at the pancakes. Dad had shaped them to look like Slimer from *Ghostbusters*.

"Too soon?" Dad asked.

Whether or not Dad had intended it as a joke, I couldn't stop laughing. He smiled in relief and ruffled my hair.

"Don't encourage him, honey," Mom told Dad. "He'll grow up to be some sort of ghost hunter or something."

"Don't worry," Sophie said through a mouth packed with pancakes. "When I grow up I want to be an auditor."

This time, Mom was the one who couldn't stop laughing.

"You don't want to be a horse trainer?" Dad asked sarcastically.

"Nope," Sophie said. "I wonder why?" she added with a smile.

I was happy right then. Really happy. We'd been through a lot but we could already laugh about it. I still missed my hometown, but as long as we had each other, we'd be okay no matter what life threw at us.

After all, Sophie and I had beat a ghost, a ghost horse, *and* a woman who wanted us dead. After they'd arrived and arrested Clara, we'd told the police everything, even about the ghosts. Who knows if they'd believed us? But they'd recorded our statements and told us they'd investigate whether or not Clara had anything to do with killing Danny and Jack. Two days later there was an article in the paper that said Clara had confessed and would be tried for their murders in addition to what she had done to us. I finished eating my Slimer pancakes and cleared my plate and cutlery, leaving Sophie, Mom, and Dad at the table. The Sunday newspaper was on the counter beside the sink. A headline caught my eye, and I froze. My plate nearly slipped out of my fingers. I hurriedly put my dishes away, grabbed the newspaper off the counter, tucked it into the back of my pants, and concealed it with my shirt.

No one had noticed what I'd done.

"Hey, um, Sophie?" I said. "Do you still have that Batman comic of mine?"

"Yeah?"

"Can I have it back?"

"Sure."

"Now?"

Sophie sighed and stood from her chair. "Fine."

Mom stared at me with a raised eyebrow and then looked at Dad.

He shrugged and said, "When a boy's gotta read Batman, a boy's gotta read Batman."

I led Sophie upstairs, my feet heavy and my head spinning. She tried to go to her room to get the comic but I guided her into mine.

"The comic's in—"

"I don't need the comic." I said. I peeked at my closet. All week I'd been casting nervous glances at it even though I knew Danny had gone to the Netherrealm and wouldn't be back.

"What's wrong?" Sophie asked.

I pulled the newspaper out from behind my shirt. "Remember how Clara said Shade and her father died with unfinished business and came back for revenge?"

Sophie nodded slowly, her eyes widening.

I pointed to the article that had caught my eye in the kitchen.

The headline read: COURTICE MURDER SUSPECT CLARA CREIGHTON DIES OF HEART ATTACK.

"If she doesn't have unfinished business *and* a thirst for revenge," I said as a chill nearly as cold as Ernest's death touch spread through my body, "I don't know who does."

ABOUT THE AUTHOR

© Colleen Morris

Joel A. Sutherland is the author of *Be a Writing Superstar*, numerous volumes of the Haunted Canada series (which have received the Silver Birch Award and the Hackmatack Award), and *Frozen Blood*, a horror novel that was nominated for the Bram Stoker Award. His short fiction has appeared in many anthologies and magazines, including *Blood Lite II & III* and *Cemetery Dance* magazine, alongside the likes of Stephen King and Neil Gaiman. He has been a juror for the John Spray Mystery Award and the Monica Hughes Award for Science Fiction and Fantasy.

He is a Children's and Youth Services Librarian and appeared as "The Barbarian Librarian" on the Canadian edition of the hit television show *Wipeout*, making it all the way to the third round and proving that librarians can be just as tough and wild as anyone else.

Joel lives with his family in southeastern Ontario, where he is always on the lookout for ghosts.

Read all the books in the Haunted series!

HAUNTED

The Nightmare Next Door

Joel A. Sutherland

HAUNTED

Field of Screams

Joel A. Sutherland

HAUNTED

Ghosts Never Die

Joel A. Sutherland

HAUNTED

Night of the Living Dolls

Joel A. Sutherland